OFF THE RECORD

OFF THE RECORD

JOCELYN QUINN

NEW DEGREE PRESS

OFF THE RECORD

ISBN 978-1-63676-572-3 *Paperback*
978-1-63676-173-2 *Kindle Ebook*
978-1-63676-174-9 *Ebook*

To my mom, Susanna Quinn.
You shooed death away
with your middle finger.
Everything I am is because of you.

CONTENTS

AUTHOR'S NOTE

October 9, 2014, was the first time I felt taken seriously. I came downstairs, as I regularly did, for dessert at one of my mother's Off The Record media dinners. She would gather eight to ten female journalists and a prominent political figure for a personal dinner at our house. All conversation was allowed, but not to be printed. At the head of the table at this dinner sat a governor and eventual presidential candidate.

My entrance to the dinner was often the same. Mom would introduce me, and everyone would smile, and then I would take my seat and eat my cake while the grown-ups talked. But this time was different. The governor turned to me and asked, "So Jocelyn, what are you interested in?" I set my fork down and went for the first thing I could think of which didn't make me sound like a child.

"Music," I said, "rock 'n' roll, specifically."

The governor smiled and asked, "Do you play any instruments?" I had been trying to learn the guitar for four years with a 1940s Yamaha I had forced my mother to keep when my aunt passed away.

"No, but I do have a guitar, upstairs."

The governor looked at my mother for a sign of permission, and then said, "Would you mind getting it?"

When I returned with the guitar, everyone had moved from the dining room table to the living room couches. I handed the governor the guitar, and he played for thirty minutes while talking to me about my favorite artists. In a room full of powerful and articulate journalists, the governor had seen me and we were talking about Led Zeppelin.

I realized much later, as I sat down to write this book, I have been chasing the feeling of being "taken seriously" ever since. It's not a lot to ask for, when you think about it. I just wanted to be seen as someone who was capable, someone who could do whatever they put their mind to. The governor had looked at me and seen a brain, opinions, and meaning in those opinions.

In Washington DC, where I was born and raised, it's no secret the air we breathe is filled with political conversation. Thus, I have always been interested in politics. I never wanted to be a politician, but I have always wanted to write about them. So, while most kids my age were focused on Zayn leaving One Direction, I was keeping up with who held the House and Senate majority. Nerd alert, I know.

From my mother's media dinners and Washington's "this for that" mentality, I learned from a young age that life is all about connections: who you know, how you know them, and most importantly, *if you can quote them.*

When I was five years old, my parents brought me to a Democratic Campaign Committee breakfast in Colorado before a long day of skiing. I plopped myself down at a table with a pile of pancakes and scarfed them down while my parents made their way around the room.

After a few minutes alone, an older man came over and sat next to me. "And what is your name?" he asked sweetly.

"Jocelyn," I replied confidently, cutting pancake bites with the side of my plastic fork. We sat there and talked for a while about whatever you can talk for a while about with a five-year-old. When my mother approached, she was half-laughing and half-grinning from ear to ear. The gentlemen was Congressman Steny Hoyer. At the time, he was the Democratic Minority Whip.

When we got home from our trip, I wrote Mr. Hoyer to tell him I enjoyed our probably riveting conversation and at the end of the note I scribbled in red color pencil, "My mom said the Democrats have tough races ahead and you need money. It's okay, I am losing lots of teeth. P.S. I never win races, I am way too slow." Along with the note, I gave him my tooth fairy money: two dollars.

Steny and I are pen pals to this day. Corresponding with him always maintained my interests in politics. Before long, I realized I wanted to do what so many women around me are doing: write about it.

In my experience, the female journalists I know are just as ambitious, if not more, than their male counterparts. They have to be. But every so often, especially during this polarizing presidency, I see news headlines showing a female journalist getting mocked or disrespected for simply doing her job.

I know I may not see the end of this disrespect in my lifetime.

When I started to polish the plot of this book, I realized I was taking the desire to be taken seriously, the exhaustion of having to prove myself, and flat-out anger, and using it all to fuel Liz's character.

Ambition, fueled by frustration, allowed me to create a strong protagonist who isn't afraid to uncover truths and push boundaries, and most importantly, stand up for herself. I hope you will relate to her and her journey and enjoy reading this book as much as I enjoyed writing it. Bonus points if you can find all the music references!

Enjoy,
Jocelyn

CHAPTER

ONE

"Give me a place to stand and I will move the world."

—*ARIANNA HUFFINGTON*

Crying in Starbucks is never a good idea.

It usually means your day is already going to shit before you've even had your morning coffee, and that you have to keep your sunglasses on inside. In my case, it was a 4 p.m. coffee, and I could barely see through my tears let alone my scratched-up Ray-Ban lenses.

Still, I could argue by any other family's standards I was handling things quite well. It's not like I made a habit of crying in coffeehouses throughout metropolitan Washington. The last time I remembered bawling in public was fifteen years ago while saying goodbye to my mother in a downtown parking lot before boarding a camp bus. But now my mother had left me, and gone a lot farther than Maine.

I wiped my tears with the back of my thumb, careful not to spill the coffee that would get me through a long night of waiting tables, and dragged myself a few doors down to the surf 'n' turf bar I call home. Since Mom passed away almost a month ago, working at Millies is my greatest distraction. By work, I mean memorizing the neighborhood moms' salad orders and humming along to the Billy Joel playing in the background, all while trying not to break a sweat. Summer in Washington DC is like the eleventh plague—so muggy that if Congress didn't take a recess in August, the Capitol would probably go up in flames.

When I opened the back door to the kitchen, I was met with a gust of heat from the stoves and the smell of sizzling shrimp.

"Dizzy Miss Lizzie! You ready for the Saturday night rush?" I knew it was Christian, the general manager, before I even saw his face. "I have some good news for you," he continued. "You're behind the bar tonight," which stopped me in my tracks. I'd been begging him to bartend forever.

"Brian called in sick, and you're the only one in here who knows how to make drinks! You'll have someone else back there to help out. It's no different than serving. You just have to stay in one place. Think you can handle that?"

"As long as I can play music and someone else cuts the fruit!" I hollered back as I headed for the bar. I could hear his famous chuckle, and I took it as his blessing.

As I examined the pint glasses and bottles of liquor, I nibbled on my lip to dull my grin. I started at Millies in high school and felt like I had been serving forever. The bar is different because you make more and the work is faster, so you aren't held to the same standards of manners and etiquette as a server. Plus, I could probably sneak a drink here and there.

"Did you finally blackmail Chris into giving you a chance behind the bar?" said Brandon. He'd been at Millies almost as long as I had and was everyone's favorite bartender. On lunch breaks he would show me how to pour cocktails and change taps.

"Apparently I'm the only one in here who knows how to make drinks," I teased, tossing a bar rag in his direction.

"Don't you start that new job on Monday?"

"Yeah, but just because I'll have my fancy journalism job doesn't mean I'm leaving my favorite place behind."

It wasn't entirely fancy. Monday was my first day as a junior investigative journalist at *The District*, a news media company based in DC that was more literally a newspaper with some online articles.

"The day you leave Millies is the day I win the lottery," he mumbled, and I nodded in agreement. "Tonight's gonna be busy, we have a big group reserved for the patio, and it's basically the first weekend of the summer."

Weekends are always busy, the kind of busy that makes me forget about Mom. As I pulled wine glasses from the dishwasher and stacked them behind me, my first bar customer approached—a middle-aged woman with red stained lips reminding me of my grandmother's.

"Hi honey, can I get two Frosès? And two of the Fisherman tacos—whatever you call 'em."

Millies' frozen rosè, or Frosè, is our staple. It's a dangerous mix of vodka, rosè, and sugar—you only have to drink one, but no one ever stops there. It was one of Mom's favorite things, and she even requested I bring her home some in a kid's cup a few times.

"Two Frosès and two Fisher's Landing tacos—you got it." I took her card and entered everything into the computer, already grateful the customers had to come to me instead of the other way around.

"I can't believe I even like those tacos," she said, reapplying the lip stain she definitely didn't need. "I mean who would think to put scallops and bacon inside a taco?"

"That's Chef for you," I smiled, "he has a way of putting things together that shouldn't work—but delicious, isn't it?"

"It's wonderful! And like everything in this city, overpriced." She winked at me and took her drinks over to a bar table. She was right, but I've always believed people spend the money for the Millies experience rather than just the food.

Anxious to escape the dust of piling papers and fundraising phone calls on The Hill, Washingtonians trade their linen suits and Ferragamo platforms for Vineyard Vines slacks and sundresses to grace the dive-bar-slash-beach-shack. Millies is like a drug to the locals. Once they sit down, they stay for hours and spend a lot.

As Brandon poured the drink mixes into their mixing machines, I scanned the bar area looking for something to do. Lady Lip Stain was approached by a handsome male friend. *If she and her red stained lips can find a man,* I thought, *you and your Burt's Bees should be able to. I* took my hair down and reapplied my chap-stick. Aside from these two and a few golf guys watching TV, most of the bar was empty. Five o'clock is always a weird time at Millies. For some it's almost dinnertime, yet some are still drinking from lunch.

It took until around 7:30 p.m. for the bar to pick up. Customers filed in from all directions, and when every seat had been filled, I looked at Brandon with a nervous smile.

"You got this," he mouthed from the other side of the bar.

When I finally got a moment to breathe, it was ten o'clock. Something about being on my feet for six hours makes the excitement of Millies fade, and my desire to sit down with a beer excruciating. I rolled my ankles and stared at the computer screen, trying to remember what the heck I was doing there.

"Is this seat open?" *No, it's reserved for my patience.*

"First come first serve!" I hollered behind me as I closed out a tab. The metal chair legs screeched against the floor and I heard a body plop into it. I tried to guess what his order would be. It was probably an IPA, but in this town I don't put it beyond men to order Rosé.

"A tequila shot and a Stella when you get a chance." *That's bold.*

"Must be celebrating," I forced a smile as I grabbed the Jose Quervo and whisked around to begin pouring.

"In fact, I am." When I looked up, my eyes widened at his strong chin and green eyes—to my surprise, he was not old. Had to be at least thirty-two, but definitely not a day over forty. I almost over poured the shot glass but habit kicked in.

"Oh? What do you do?"

He stared at me for a moment as if he wasn't sure how to answer, which could mean anything from unemployed to working in the CIA. He continued to stare, and suddenly I felt uncomfortable.

"Sorry," I said, "that was such a Washington question. In Manhattan, you're defined by your net worth, in DC, it's your job."

"In that case, I'll give you a Washington answer," he said with a broad smile. Then he leaned in toward me. "I'm kind of a recovering lawyer," he said, those eyes only inches from my own. "I started working at a New York law firm a few months ago. I hated it. Keeping track of tenths of hours, spending way too much time at work, wishing all the while I had gone to business school. If you practice law in New York, you pretty quickly wish you were an investment banker. Of course, if you're an investment banker, you wish you ran a hedge fund. If you run a hedge fund, you wish you were a private equity titan. Bruce Springsteen, you know?"

I nodded and our eyes met, "*Badlands*."

"Exactly," he grinned, seemingly impressed I understood the reference. I realized being a host at Millies was like starting at the bottom peg of the poor man in the song—making bartenders kings. I had to say something to maintain his interest, but I thought it better not to mention today was my first day behind the bar.

"Washington's no different," I said. "No one is content here. House members want to be senators, and senators think they should be president. Maybe that's just the human condition."

"Is that a good thing or a bad thing?" he smirked. He was mischievous, but not in a gross way—like you will love him until you hate yourself.

"It's always okay to want more," he said, "but the problem with more money or more power is it leads to wanting even more of both. It's like an addiction that can never be satiated." I nodded and hoped he couldn't tell I was utterly and completely checking him out. He had trimmed dark hair, shorter on the sides than the top, and slicked over like Don Draper's in *Mad Men*. He wore a pristine, dark grey suit, and his eyes were like emerald pools begging me to dive in. He was dreamy, like the high school quarterback when you're a freshman—but with a brain. I found myself glad he had taken the chair reserved for my patience.

The aforementioned Saturday night rush was picking up, which meant that while I wanted to stand there talking about Bruce and the human condition, I had a bar of thirsty Washingtonians to tend to. I headed over where two men in dark colored golf polos sat at the very end of bar just before the patio begins. When it looked like they weren't quite ready to order, I stalled by getting silverware and water glasses. One of them leaned back, putting his arm on the chair of the other,

"So Bill," he began, adjusting his baseball cap, "What are they saying about DUST in your office?"

Bill, apparently, chuckled, as they both eyed *Sports Center* behind me. "That it's a damn good way to put us in tough negotiating spots overseas."

I knew they were referring to the DUST Act, or Defending US Troops Act, which had recently passed in the House. It was about increased defense contracting for the US military.

"It'll sure as hell bring money to DC," Ron responded, "and I can practically see the Raytheon and Boeing buildings from here."

"Maybe," Bill said, "but it's a conservative move for Salina after winning all those swing states," he declared, and I agreed.

President Salina ran on the Republican ticket, but won with a few swing states due to his moderate policies. I didn't know much beyond that since I had only regained the energy to watch the news a few weeks prior, in an effort to get ready for *The District*.

It occurred to me Millies might be the last place in Washington where the playful bipartisanship my grandfather always talked about still existed. But then I thought of all the underground bars in downtown hotels where the people of my parents' generation gathered, and realized I was just being cynical.

I approached the two gentlemen when it seemed their conversation had come to a pause. "Can I get you all something to drink?"

"I'll have a Shark Tracker, thanks," said one. I turned to the other.

"Whatever that champagne beer is you guys have on tap," he said, squinting at the row of beer tap handles.

After setting the beers down, I walked back toward Mr. Emerald Eyes to see a credit card sitting on the counter.

"So, what's your Washington answer?" he asked, carefully examining my name plate.

"It's Liz." I smiled, "and I asked you first!"

"Okay. A little of everything," he said, his eyes twinkling. "I keep the trains running on time, or at least I try to. Nothing a hundred other people haven't done." His phone began to ring.

"As a matter of fact, I have to go make sure two trains don't crash right now." I felt the exhilaration of our conversation come to a halt. But to my surprise, he silenced the phone.

"Your turn."

I tried to hide my delight, "Let's just say I'm the one who writes about those trains you mentioned."

"Well, Liz," he said as his phone rang again. "It was nice to meet you, and good luck with the trains." As he picked up the call, I hollered, "you too!" and that was the end of that. Mr. Emerald Eyes was leaving, and I had hours of beer pouring and tip counting ahead.

CHAPTER

TWO

"I have always said 'yes' to opportunities and experiences."

—NORAH O'DONNELL

My Sunday morning hangover reminded me just because you're offered a drink doesn't mean you should accept it.

Granny had let herself in and entered the bedroom with coffee and confrontation.

She had been beautiful when she was young and was never required to be much else. She was painfully old fashioned, so the idea of me working at all, let alone two jobs, was provocative. Granny lost her own mom to cancer when she was a child, resulting in an intense desire to be in control which drove her first husband away and her second husband to the bottle. After my mother died, I became the focus of her oversight. But she adored me, and I adored her.

"Darling, why must you horse around at that bar on the weekends when this job will put you right in the epicenter of eligible bachelors? I'm sure you'll be the only woman," she boasted with disappointment.

I tried to contain my laughter as I imagined my mother saying, "She's such a WASP!"

"Granny, what's the harm in extra money?" I groaned.

"Elizabeth, by the time I was your age I was married with your mother on the way." I bit my tongue to avoid noting her first marriage was a failure and we were no longer living in the previous century. "If you must work, you should at least dress to catch attention," she said, rifling through my mother's closet.

I didn't need the money. I needed Millies. I needed a job that didn't feel like it was handed to me. A place where the Mason name and the week-day suit chaffing could hide under khaki shorts and hard-earned tips.

Bennett Mason was a famous broadcast journalist in Washington during the 1960s and 1970s. Lucky for me, he was also my grandfather, Granny's first husband, whom I called GP. He grew up in Oklahoma and moved to Washington to start his journalism career after graduating Dartmouth. He and Granny met in a hotel lobby while she waited for a cab. When he asked her on a date, she accused him of being too forward. I guess he liked the chase. There wasn't much I remembered about GP, except his laugh could make the floors shake and he loved Dr Pepper. Everyone in this town knows the name Bennett Mason.

The District's founder William O'Donnell is also from Oklahoma, and GP was on TV when O'Donnell was in diapers. In the week before she passed, Mom had mustered up the energy to call O'Donnell and appeal to his Oklahoma roots to get me an interview. It was her way of making sure I was taken care of after she departed this earth.

The only thing I knew about O'Donnell's office was his managing director, Tim Marshall, was very busy. In my interview—which was less like an interview and more like a handshake—he only managed to get out a few words in between phone calls.

"So, you can write?" he asked.

"Yes, all kinds of writing. I can show you some of my—"

"When can you start?" he interrupted. And that was that.

Granny pushed around hanger after hanger, and I couldn't tell anymore if my hangover was giving me a headache or if it was the screeching sound of metal on metal.

"I'm sure Eleanor has *something* in here you can wear that your femininity won't drown in."

I knew Mom's closet like the back of my hand. In fact, I stole her clothes so often over the years she started checking my outfits when I left the house. But now things were different. It became too hard to feel her clothes and smell her perfume after she was gone, so I avoided the closet. While it was occasionally upsetting to sleep in a house she no longer did, I had to get back on my feet before any moving was to be done.

"She has those Luigi suits." I groaned, pulling my hair into a sad excuse of a bun and joining her search. I knew if they were here they'd be hiding behind the gowns she wore to the Meridian Balls and State Dinners. She was taller than me, and thinner than me, and I could hear her saying, "Thank god we're the same shoe size." They would have to be tailored to fit, (note to self: call Luigi's) but there was nothing I wanted more than the protective shield of Eleanor Mason's suits to protect me from the impending judgment of fellow staffers who did not get the job because of their grandfather.

Most fashion-forward Washington women get their pricey L'agence and Valentino wardrobes from Bloomingdales or Saks. But Granny and Mom had Luigi. I think he was the brother of the cousin of the husband of Granny's former housekeeper. His wife had died shortly before she met him many years ago, and he supported his young son by sewing hemlines in a basement apartment in Southeast—a neighborhood my grandmother consciously avoided. I firmly believed, since she rarely stepped foot out of the three-square miles around her house, Granny still believed Washington was how it used to be.

Before long, Luigi went from sewing buttons on my Grandfather's shirts to copying clothes straight out of Vogue and tailoring them perfectly for Granny. When the ladies at the club asked where she found such beautiful pieces, she finally revealed his identity to her friends.

Suddenly, everyone wanted a Luigi original. He had become astronomically expensive for everyone but Granny, and he'd made my mother a better wardrobe than some of the most glamorous women in Washington. Leaving it behind for me to wear as I started my not-so-glamorous job of junior investigative journalism. But it was a job after all, and I couldn't bartend forever.

"Granny, look, they're fabulous," I said as I unveiled one suit after another.

"Oh wow," she said. "It's been a long time since I've seen these. I had them made for your mother when she decided to glue herself to a desk chair instead of getting married."

The truth was Granny had set Mom up with the son of one of her ladies at the club. After one lunch together, she brushed him off as a "stuck up prick" and interviewed for the position of a Senate staffer. Granny still held a grudge about it. I watched as she unhooked one of the jackets to check the inside.

"Here it is. Luigi's trademark stitch."

A beautiful cursive EM by Luigi was sewn right into the jacket, just below the collar. Without missing a beat, Granny showed me the inside of her own jacket, bearing an MM by Luigi.

It's a funny thing to remember your grandparents have real names, like Martha Mason. As Granny transferred Mom's gowns to the back of the closet and the suits to the front, I wondered what a young Eleanor Mason was feeling on the day before her first job.

Mom was in no way the debutante daughter Granny had wanted, but she was plenty of steps closer than me. She cursed like a trucker but always had pink lip gloss on, and she could chug a beer faster than anyone but she would never tell you. When Granny and Bennett got a divorce, Mom was forced to become strictly independent at age twelve.

While Mom rebelled personality-wise, her jobs were always in line with what Granny saw as acceptable for a woman. After college she worked as a Senate aide, then a real estate agent, then she wrote for a few magazines, until she decided to utilize the Mason heritage for hosting media dinners with female journalists and prominent political figures. Counting my nervous thoughts, I hoped some of her confidence would rub off on me after a few days wearing the Luigi originals.

"You never know, Granny, plenty of the men I'll run into while covering stories on The Hill will grace my presence at Millies, too." I knew it would calm her century-old anxieties, and I wasn't lying. Millies draws the younger version of the crowds at The Capital Grille and The Hay Adams, and a lot of them have trust funds and Gucci loafers, but there's always the odd one out.

Once my wardrobe was figured out, Granny told me to "put my face on" and that she'd left a grocery list on the kitchen counter. The woman rarely left the house at all, and much less to buy her own groceries. When she did, she never went without makeup. She was constantly scribbling her grocery lists and writing things down so she wouldn't forget to tell me. Things like, "Rock Hudson made a pass at me at the Polo Lounge in Beverly Hills." She had told me that story more than twenty times. I always acted as if it was a secret she was sharing for the first time. I never mentioned her late second husband told me it was actually a very drunk Granny who made a pass at a very gay Rock Hudson.

After I walked her to the door, I summoned the energy to haul it back up the stairs. My phone was buzzing on the bedside table, and I prayed it was not another distant relative calling about my mother.

"Hello?" I said, unable to hold off a yawn.

"Morning sunshine! Miss me?"

"Casey!" I screamed. "Where have you been?"

Casey was my first and best friend at Millies. She was almost exactly two-and-a-half years older than me, which didn't matter now, but when we first met she was a junior in college and I hadn't even started. We were both hosts at the time, and to be frank, she scared the hell out of me. She had the darkest brown eyes I had ever seen—almost black. She could get away with anything on the job, and even the kitchen staff let her make her own lunch. The kitchen staff didn't like anyone. She drank pretty much every night of the week, and never turned down a night out. After a few weeks hosting together, I learned she is the way she is because she doesn't give a rat's ass about what people think of her. It's intimidating, unless she's on your side.

"Oh don't worry about it," was her classic response. "What's important is I'm coming back! I get in tomorrow. Meet me at Millies?"

"Sure, I have work probably until five or six," I guessed.

"I'll just come in at the end of your shift!" She sounded hyper. Which, at 10 a.m., wasn't beyond her.

"Not Millies, it's my first day at a new desk job—monkey suit and all," I said as I gazed at the Luigi originals.

"Oh! You have to tell me all about it tomorrow over drinks."

I laughed, "Of course. But seriously, how are you?" Casey had left a few weeks prior with the drummer in a band headed for Nashville. I was in no position to stop her, having just lost Mom, so no one did.

"I'm great!" she exclaimed. "Nashville was the best time. We gotta go together."

"And the guy? What about him?"

"Easy come easy go," she responded, changing the subject. "What about you? Any guys?"

"Little busy over here, Case, not exactly in the mood to date."

"Oh come on," she sighed, " not anyone?"

Telling her about Mr. Emerald Eyes at the bar felt like telling someone your wish after you blow out birthday candles. Just wrong. But I knew she'd get a kick out of it.

"Well, there was this guy who came into Millies last night. Seemed smart, and he was movie-star handsome. We talked about Bruce Springsteen. But I don't even know his name," I shrugged.

"Doesn't matter," she declared, "he knows where you work! And you've always managed to look better in that awful polo than anyone. I wish I had boobs."

I laughed, "Call me when you and your flat chest are back in DC."

"We will," she said confidently, and clicked off.

Casey had said only one thing to me when Mom died: "You're going to be alright, more than alright. That's what Eleanor would have wanted." She hadn't mentioned it since. Not because she didn't care, but because emotion wasn't really her strong suit. It was actually refreshing, after weeks of nothing but emotion.

I could have gotten back in bed and stayed there all day. But I knew it would only make me feel worse. Plus, Granny would call and wake me up soon enough if I didn't bring over her groceries. I had an anxiety-induced habit of doing two things at once while getting ready, whether it was brushing my teeth while making my bed, or in this case, texting.

Brandon (1)

Good luck tomorrow big shot. Do what everyone else here does and assume you know nothing. But for God's sake, don't act like it.

I laughed, choking on toothpaste, and conjured up a witty response.

Oh please. You know I'm a terrible actor.

CHAPTER THREE

"Women, whatever their profession, tend to have a harder time feeling ready for a job, even though in most cases they are more than prepared."

—DANA BASH

Tim Marshall, *The District's* managing director, didn't seem to remember me.

He barely even noticed me as I leaped from a chair in the lobby. I had arrived fifteen minutes before nine in my first choice of three Eleanor Mason suits, had time to get Starbucks, and found a parking space in the section of the garage marked for *The District*. It was three floors below a beautiful office building, two doors down from the Mayflower Hotel.

The District's seventh floor office was not a big room with thirty cubicles and paper clutter like I had expected. Instead, the elevators opened to a large front lobby with a reception desk toward the back, and a beautiful painting on the open wall space. It had big glass doors behind a seating area which opened to a large conference room. As I sipped my double-shot soy latte, the elevator dinged and opened.

"Did you call O'Donnell's home?" Tim barked at the receptionist.

She jumped to her feet, but before she could say anything, he pivoted around and clamped a hand on the shoulder of a short, wiry young man who looked like an intern hurrying past him.

"Did you check the gym?"

"I called the front desk and—"

"I didn't ask you to call the front desk. I asked you to check the gym. Go check the gym. Now!"

The man dashed toward the elevators, and Tim turned his attention back to the receptionist. "Wendy, I'm still waiting for an answer to my question."

"I'm sorry, Tim," Wendy mumbled, avoiding eye contact.

"I want an answer, Wendy. Not an apology. An answer."

"His wife said he left two hours ago to drop their daughter off at school."

"Did she get to school on time?"

"I called her and left a message, and she just texted me back."

"What did she say?" he asked with growing agitation.

Wendy hesitated. "'Geometry's boring.'"

Tim looked like he was going to throw something at her. Instead, he crumpled a piece of paper in his hand. "Leave another message for O'Donnell, and let me know the moment you hear from him." He turned and headed toward the hallway. If I was going to get his attention, it was now or never.

"Tim!" I called out, a little more urgently than I intended, "Hi, behind you, um, it's Liz Mason, today is my first day."

I swear his shoulders seemed to rise in displeasure as he turned around.

"I was just wondering if you could tell me where I'm supposed to work?" I asked.

He greeted me with clenched teeth, and I couldn't help but stare at the veins popping out of his forehead.

"Wendy, could you please show Ms. Mason where her desk is located."

"You told me to call Mr. O'Donnell," Wendy said, jumping to her feet again.

"First, call him. Then show Liz to her desk. Got it?" With that, he stomped away. I bunched the fabric of Mom's suit as if it could magically turn me invisible. After the phone call went to voicemail and she let out a deep sigh, Wendy motioned for me to follow her. Behind the reception desk, the lobby opened up to a hallway going in both directions. As we turned the right corner, I could hear her stick heels mashing against the broadloom carpet.

"Hi, Wendy, I'm Liz. Thank you," I said, trying to make eye contact while keeping up with her.

"Sorry about Tim," she said, slowing her pace, "He's just stressed out because we're supposed to run a piece on the secretary of state pick and O'Donnell hasn't okay-ed it yet. He'll warm up to you."

"I understand. It seems like work here is exciting. The office sure is nice."

Wendy stopped in front of an empty cubicle on the left of the hallway, "Yeah, O'Donnell used to be a partner at a law firm here—a big one. He didn't want to get rid of the space and didn't want to retire either, so here we are." I laughed, and she smiled.

"This is where you will be working, across from you are the big kids—the senior writers—and down the hall is Tim."

"So, does Mr. O'Donnell check every piece that runs on the site?" I asked, placing my bag on the floor and sitting in the unforgivably squeaky desk chair.

"Not at all, but this one is big. We have the scoop on not only who Salina has picked, but why he's firing the current secretary."

Names had been flying around on the news in the past week or so for who President Salina was picking for the new secretary of state. Rumor was Salina was not satisfied with the work done in his first one hundred days, and neither were his party leaders. Salina was cleaning house. He recently replaced his chief of staff, right after the senior counselor quit.

"I think it's Congressman Bonham," I said quietly. House Minority Leader Greg Bonham had the strongest background in foreign policy out of all the names I heard, and his nickname was "The Mallet" because he had a big head but the force of experience to back it.

"I see," I continued, "and is Tim also the White House correspondent?"

"We don't have one yet. Tim has friends in the administration. I think O'Donnell is tired of mornings like these, so that's why we've been hiring more," Wendy said, nodding unpleasantly in Tim's direction.

I bit my tongue, knowing I was in no position to judge anyone yet.

Wendy handed me a manila folder filled with papers. "Boss told me to give you this—a welcome packet I guess—he should be in shortly, but for now just make yourself at home. Kitchen is down the hall on the left, and bathrooms are by the elevator."

"Thank you, Wendy," I said, placing the folder next to a desktop computer which was no doubt from 2005, complete with a plug-in mouse and keyboard.

The first item in the folder was a contract stating my job description and FLSA rights, which I quickly signed. Behind it was a non-disclosure agreement, which I didn't have to read thoroughly to understand it basically said to keep my mouth shut about *The District's* newsworthy information. It did make me sit up a bit straighter, realizing I would be working with information the public didn't yet have.

"You must be Liz," a taller, dark haired guy chimed in from the cubicle next to mine.

"I am, and you are?"

"Derek. Have you met the warden yet?" he smiled. "I mean, Tim?"

"I think he would notice a fly on the wall before me, but yes."

As I filed through the remainder of the papers, I heard Wendy's voice barreling down the hall.

"Tim! O'Donnell's on line two!"

Derek grabbed his landline and whispered, "Pick up line two and press mute." I wasn't sure if he was serious.

"That's eavesdropping," I whispered back.

"It's the only way to know what the hell's going on around here," he hissed. I did as told, picking up in time to hear Tim sounding like O'Donnell's angry girlfriend.

"Where are you?"

"On my way," was O'Donnell's nonchalant response.

"We have twenty minutes if we want to beat *Politico* and the rest of them."

"Tim, have you had more than one coffee already? I'm just around the corner," said O'Donnell, and I imagined Tim's head literally exploding. But he responded calmly.

"Boss, with all due respect, it's not every day we get the leaked list of the president's top picks for secretary of state."

"Oh! How's Bennett Mason's granddaughter doing?" O'Donnell said, ignoring Tim's "due respect." The skin on my neck prickled.

"Don't worry about it," Tim said.

"I'm not. I just want to know how she's doing."

"She's doing nothing because she knows nothing."

I wanted to hide, but that wasn't an option in my very transparent and open cubicle.

"She thinks she knows how things work because Grandpa talked about it at Christmas dinner."

"Listen, Tim, she's got potential. She's a good writer, and her mother's the one who chaired all those Off The Record media dinners with countless senators and even a fucking secretary of state."

"Well, fine. What do you want to put her on then?"

"I haven't decided. But give the girl a break, her mother just passed away a month ago. It's gotta be hard."

"We're giving her a break by giving her the job. What—now you want me at her desk, tissues in hand?"

I hung up. I had heard enough. Derek continued to listen raptly, and I resisted the temptation to rip the receiver out of his hands. In an effort to hide my frustration, knowing full-well Derek was about to lose respect for me, I continued flipping through the welcome packet.

The first words I saw were "White House Correspondents Association." As I scanned the page, I realized it was an application for a press pass. O'Donnell just told Tim he hadn't decided what to put me on. This could not be it. The White House?

"Elizabeth Mason! Welcome to the club." I quickly closed the folder to look up and see O'Donnell himself.

"Please, sir, call me Liz. It's nice to finally meet you."

He crossed his arms over the top of my cubicle window, "I see Wendy gave you the folder."

"Oh yes, I was just finishing up the contracts. Is there someone I need to bring them to?"

"I'll take care of it. Come on down to my office and we can discuss all the details."

O'Donnell was not what I expected. I had seen pictures when I Googled him, and I knew from Wendy and my cyber stalking he was somewhat of a lobbying legend—but I was not expecting Mr. Nice Guy. He escorted me back down the hall to the office nearest the lobby.

"Wait here, I have to check in with Tim before he loses it."

"No problem. Thank you, sir."

After finding a seat on the brown leather couch which looked like it belonged in a senator's office, I started to feel a sense of belonging. O'Donnell's office was beautiful. He had four TVs on the right wall, each with a different news channel on. *CNN* and *Fox* on the top two, *Bloomberg* and *MSNBC* on the bottom.

I had a hunch O'Donnell himself wasn't entirely left-leaning like *The District* seemed to be, but I also knew GP watched every channel himself to chuckle at each network's spin on the headline of the day. The Masons have always been Democrats, even in Oklahoma.

Across from me were two rich blue velvet lounge chairs and behind them a shiny reddish-wooden desk bigger than my entire cubicle. Behind the large desk was a smaller one, pushed up against the window and housing O'Donnell's desktop, seemingly not from 2005. I imagined having an office like his one day, swiveling around from the desktop computer to greet inferiors like myself. Just like in Badlands, I thought. Mr. Emerald Eyes would laugh.

Just as I caught myself smiling, O'Donnell barreled through the door.

"Alright Liz, you have a pen and paper?" He took his jacket off and wiped a small bit of sweat from his forehead before sitting across from me. Shit. I didn't have anything.

"No sir, I don't actually, I can go get one if—"

"No problem, you can use your phone." I took out my phone and opened up notes. "I hope you saw more than just the contracts in the folder I gave you," he said, resting his elbows on the chair's arms.

"I did, sir, and forgive me but I'm a bit confused. I'm covering the White House?"

He chuckled lowly. "I thought you would say that. I haven't discussed it with Tim yet," lowering his voice and leaning in, he added, "He's a bit skeptical of your journalistic abilities, but I know you're familiar with how this town works. Bennett Mason was a role model of mine and your mother was an impressive woman. I'm sorry she's no longer with us."

"Thank you, she's the reason I want to be a journalist actually—she always made sure I was informed."

"And it shows," he said, standing up to sit behind his desk. "Which is why I believe you are cut-out for the West Wing. I read the pieces you sent in with your application. You're a smart writer. And you need people skills for it. I'm sure Eleanor Mason raised quite the extrovert."

"Growing up here definitely has its benefits," I smiled, "I'm honored, and I can't thank you enough, Mr. O'Donnell."

"Well now, don't thank me yet," he lowered a thin pair of glasses off his forehead and clicked his desktop computer on. "Unfortunately, your first assignment will not be the most exciting part of your journey. It's a bit of a 'getting your feet wet' experience. Write this down."

"You'll be writing what we call a backgrounder. It's basically a who, what, when, and where of an event or a person. In this case, the president will be addressing the new DUST Act in the next few press conferences, so you can attend those and acquire as much information as you can." I nodded and silently recalled my eavesdropping of Ron and Bill's conversation at Millies on Saturday. Having an ear inside the Millies' regulars could actually help my investigative work. O'Donnell continued. "It's not published or anything, but it's what we use to fact-check before we publish. I figure it will get you familiar with the White House and hopefully we can get you on track to getting a hard pass in the long run."

I was furiously typing when O'Donnell took notice and waited for my thumbs to pause. He took his glasses off and leaned back steadily in his chair. "When I was a young reporter, twenty or so years ago, I saw one of your grandfather's interviews. He said in his first job in Washington, the network took a chance on him and gave him a project that started his career. Do you know what that was?" he asked.

I knew this story like the back of my hand. GP loved to tell it. "He was assigned to cover the executive order of Japanese internment camps," I said confidently, sitting up a bit straighter. "He said he'd never had so much anxiety in his life because he didn't want to speak poorly of President Roosevelt but he knew he had to 'write the wrong.'"

"Exactly," said O'Donnell, "Now, this is nothing compared to the trials of World War II, but I figure if morals run in your blood, we should put another Mason on the path to whistleblowing. You gotta start somewhere."

He stood up to escort me out and I nervously collected myself. "I won't let you down, boss."

With that he shook my hand and opened the door. "I'll need you to fill out that application. I'm waiting on approval from the press secretary, but once we get that and get you credentialed, you'll have a pass. For the next day or two, I'll have Wendy get you some good research tools." He gave me a toothy smile. "I'm excited to have you on board, Liz."

CHAPTER

FOUR

"How hard it is to learn that time with a loved one is limited and how quickly tomorrow turns into yesterday."

—*SUSANNA QUINN*

It didn't take me long to notice grief plays games with the mind.

Grief makes you forget and suppress a whole lot, but it also turns your brain onto the big picture. I had forgotten the small moments with Mom in her last few weeks with me, but I had never forgotten she would want me to be strong. She would want me to be here, at *The District,* following my journalism dreams.

Unfortunately, the timing of when those little pieces of forgotten past flew back into my brain is out of my control. And it was happening now, as I stared blankly down the hallway of my new office.

I don't remember exactly when Mom stopped eating. There weren't any dramatic gestures. It was more like she had lost interest in food, or simply forgot what she was supposed to do with it. She was on a morphine drip and drifting in and out of consciousness.

I do remember sitting by her side, trying to persuade her into taking a spoonful of sherbet. She shook her head no. She could barely speak, but her eyes pleaded with me for something. What? There was something she wanted. Something I couldn't comprehend. I asked her if she wanted water. She shook her head again, growing agitated. I felt helpless. I think I may have started to cry. "Ginger ale?" I asked. She nodded her head, and it sounds silly, but I felt ecstatic to have figured out some small way to help her. I fed her the soda through a medicine dropper, and she struggled to drink a tiny bit before pushing me away, grimacing in pain. I realized she only agreed to drink because she could tell I was upset.

The hospice nurse took my hand when I left Mom's side for a brief moment. "Even though you may have done so a hundred times before, you need to express your love and forgiveness, and that you know she forgives you. Let her know she can let go and move on."

I didn't want her to move on. But I also didn't want her to remain in pain. I sat by her bed holding her hand. Mom fought to stay awake, but the morphine made it difficult. Minutes or hours later, she woke gasping for breath. Casey was there with me, and she ran out of the room to get the nurse.

"You're a fighter, Mrs. Mason, aren't you?" she said, gently wiping Mom's lips with a glycerin swab like I'd been doing constantly. But nothing seemed to help her parched lips. "You don't need to fight so hard."

As she left the room, the nurse stopped and gripped my shoulder as if she was giving me strength.

"Mom, you've been so brave," I said to her, clasping her hand. "I had a professor who once said we don't have modern day heroes. But I do. It's you."

My mom shook her head. Her breathing got labored again; it sounded hollow. "Mom, you are brave. And I love you." I remembered all the times I had said the opposite. Like when she made me take ballet lessons. Or when we fought about me going to Dad's. It took me much too long to realize all the things she was right about. "I have always loved you."

I stopped myself from crying. This wasn't about me. This was my last chance to do something for her. "I forgive you, Mom. For anything you've ever done or didn't do." I wanted her to say the same. I imagined her having one last lucid moment. One perfect mother-daughter moment to make up for all the imperfect ones. But I knew that wasn't going to happen. "And, Mom, I know you also forgive me."

She made a face I believe was her last smile, and she left us. I don't know how I even knew. I guess it was the silence, and there was a release of tension in her body. She was at peace. I hoped she was at peace. I laid my head on her chest and began sobbing.

Instead of taking a left down the hallway and back to my desk from O'Donnell's door, I decided to take a field trip around the office. It seemed as though the decorators had perfected the lobby, conference, room, O'Donnell's office, and nothing else.

Lining the hallway walls were old framed newspaper spreads, functioning like a timeline. My first few steps were guided by World War II headlines that bore the words "invasion" and "victory" in big, dark block letters. As I continued, I briefly scanned 1950s headlines, including one about the landmark *Brown v. Board of Education* case. The most interesting artifact in what seemed to be someone's publication collection was the first *Rolling Stone* issue, bearing a young and pursed lipped John Lennon. The collection continued all the way to 9/11 headlines and the election of Barack Obama. I could have stood there closely examining each print all day.

"Cool, huh?" said Wendy, smacking her heels into the carpet as she whisked passed me.

"So cool," I replied, but she was already gone. I resumed my field trip.

The "kitchen" was the size of a coat closet (which I suspected it once was), yet a refrigerator, sink, water cooler, and Xerox machine were squeezed into the space. The combination of a major piece of electrical office equipment and water seemed like a worker's compensation case waiting to happen.

When I returned to my desk, a new stack of papers was left next to the manila folder.

"Wendy left those for you," Derek piped up, rolling his way over to me while seated in his desk chair. "You gotta get setup with Wire, too."

"Wire?"

"It's the app we use to message and store info—encrypted and all that. If you don't have any secret sources, they aren't really *your* sources."

"Oh, of course," I said, attempting to hide my confusion.

"Also, the piece about the secretary is out. You were right. It's most likely Bonham."

"Wow, do you eavesdrop on everyone?" I asked, shaking my head.

"Only the smart people," he smiled.

This job was going to take some getting used to. Not so much the research and the responsibility, just having to consistently remind myself I *belonged* here. Derek was helping, and O'Donnell said himself I'm "cut out for the West Wing."

I decided that phrase would make a great piece of décor for my lifeless desk, so I wrote it on a post-it and stuck it to the ancient computer. It was like starting a first day of school with barely any supplies.

I wasn't worried. Mom always said she wasn't a "worrier," because "worrying wouldn't change anything. Worrying is just a distraction that makes it harder to change things." She often used this excuse to stop for coffee when she was already late, but her head was in the right place.

The pile of papers included instructions on how to get set up with Wire, and having a passcode-encrypted app on my phone was one step closer to feeling like the real deal. Next were examples of backgrounders, which would help with my first assignment, and a list of some White House staff members. There were at least fifty names, all with titles having to do with communications. My eyes were first drawn to the highlighted names which indicated they were the head, or heads, of that department.

OFFICE OF THE CHIEF OF STAFF

Assistant to the President and White House Chief of Staff
- Joseph Reilly
Assistant to the President and Senior Counselor
- Cutter Levy

OFFICE OF COMMUNICATIONS

Assistant to the President and White House Director of Communications
- Dana Riviera

Assistant to the President and White House Press Secretary
- **Stephanie Patten**

I recognized only two names. The press secretary was often the focus of many TV comedy sketches, and I think the senior counselor took over recently when the former one left on maternity leave. I knew while I might get a glimpse of some of these people behind the bolded names, I would likely be rubbing shoulders with those not even listed. I was a freshman at *The District*, so naturally I would mingle with the freshmen in the White House.

After downloading Wire and following all of its prompts, I sighed and leaned back in my squeaky desk chair. My thoughts began to spiral until the anxiety made me realize I hadn't taken my Lexapro that morning. I fumbled with the orange pill bottle and used the remainder of my coffee to down two small, round pills. In a saved-by-the-bell fashion, I heard my phone buzz from the bottom of my purse.

Casey (1)
"Where is the spare key?"

I knew she meant for my house, but she hadn't asked to stay with me, so I was confused. Holding my phone under the desk, I struggled to type.

Liz: "To Mom's? In the porch light, probably swimming in dead bugs."
Casey: "I figured you could use a roommate. This place is a mess!"

Casey would undoubtedly start organizing and cleaning, and I worried she might misplace some of Mom's stuff. But she was right, I was lonely.

Liz: "Every time I try to organize I start crying!"
Casey: "I'll handle it. And no Miss OCD, I won't misplace anything."
Liz: "You read my mind. Thanks."

I barely trusted myself to deal with Mom's stuff, much less Casey. But I knew she would be careful, and I did wonder if the living room floor was still there underneath it all. In an effort to look less nervous, I began setting up the desktop computer to my liking. When I logged into my email, there was a Google alert lingering at the very top of my inbox, timestamped about fifteen minutes earlier. I'd kept them turned on for Mom and GP, as well as Millies and myself. But it had been awhile since one had popped up, probably since Mom passed away and almost every news media company in the district posted about it. There are private goodbyes and public goodbyes. Eleanor Mason required a very public goodbye.

To my surprise, the alert was about me.

GOOGLE ALERTS—ELIZABETH MASON

Daughter of late DC Queen Bee Eleanor Mason and granddaughter of Bennett Mason is hired as a new investigative journalist at The District. *Watch out, Washington, another Mason is sniffing for blood."*

—WASHINGTON ENQUIRER

I didn't have much respect for *The Washington Enquirer* after they wrote an article about Mom and called her Evelyn instead of Eleanor halfway through. At least they got my name right, and I admit I found it pretty cool I was worth a news blurb.

By lunchtime, I had successfully made the computer feel familiar and had flipped through all of the materials in the manila folder. I knew I was going to have to study up on the DUST Act until I knew it backward and forward before I even got close to the White House doors.

While her husband was stationed in Afghanistan, a worried military wife tweeted pictures of his inadequate meals and worn supplies. Since then, more people started coming out with allegations of a lack of basic resources overseas. Republicans blamed Democrat budget-cuts and Democrats blamed Russia and China.

Members from both sides of the aisle eventually proposed H.R. 426 which would "Americanize" wartime supply and prevent the United States from relying too much on foreign suppliers. The bill, if passed in the Senate, would be the president's first real victory, and he could kill two birds with one stone: strengthen the economy and support the military. After reading The Washington Post's articles on DUST, it was time to read the fine print of the bill.

Every effort should be made to ensure the adequacy of production and supply, to ensure continued cooperation between the defense and commercial sectors, and to ensure the relevant government agencies increase the sourcing of military supplies and equipment manufactured or otherwise produced by domestic American companies.

It took me a few read-overs to process, but just in time to prevent a migraine, Derek stood up to catch my attention.

"Alright, newbie," putting on his sport coat, "let's go get some lunch. There's a great place across the street. I mean, if you're not one of those chicks that only eats salad."

I laughed. If he wasn't kind of funny, I would think he was a jerk. But I was never very good at avoiding jerks, anyway. He was tall with a stern appearance and hair that was supposed to be brown, but had become awkwardly highlighted from the summer sun. "I'm more of a burger girl, I mean, if you're not one of those guys that judges a girl by what she eats."

Derek chuckled and shook his head. "Touché."

CHAPTER

FIVE

"Girls have got balls. They're just a little higher up, that's all."
—*JOAN JETT*

"Liz, your grandmother is on line three," Wendy announced down the hall just as O'Donnell bounded out from his office.

I wasn't sure why that needed to be broadcast to the entire office, but O'Donnell looked inexplicably delighted.

"May I?" he asked as he picked up my phone.

Oh, God. He probably assumed Granny was like Mom, but I didn't have time to warn him.

"Hello Mrs. Mason, this is William O'Donnell, and I wanted to personally say how sorry I am about your family's loss. My thoughts and prayers are with you. And may I add we are very lucky to have your bright granddaughter working here."

He pressed the speaker button. He wanted an audience for what he anticipated would be my grandmother's grateful response. He was in for a surprise. I sat helpless, overcome with dread for what would come out of Granny's mouth.

"Well. I don't believe that women should be forced to slave away at men's jobs, but Elizabeth has always been different. As a teenager, she spent her Friday nights at debate club instead of the Mayflower Cotillion, unlike the past five generations of women in our family. Now, I know she is busy with her very important new job, so, what did you say your name was?"

Taken aback, O'Donnell said, "Uh...William, William O'Donnell." You could have heard a pin drop in the office. *Everyone* had stopped to listen.

"Well William, I do not want you to bother Elizabeth. As I said, she is very busy, so if you could just take a quick message for me."

I prayed to somehow disappear. But O'Donnell looked amused, and Granny had certainly provided him with a great anecdote to tell his colleagues. He smiled and continued playing along, signaling Tim to take notes. I saw Derek's jaw drop in the corner of my eye.

"Yes, ma'am, I have pen in hand," O'Donnell said, nodding at Tim, "please go on."

"I need one butternut squash, a pound of green beans, romaine lettuce, and three lamb chops. Tell Elizabeth to get the lamb from the butcher. I don't want meat that has been sitting around all day. Tell her to go to Whole Foods because they have the freshest produce. But tell her she also needs to go to Giant for the rest of the list because their prices are more reasonable. I'd like a half-gallon of 1% milk, a pint of coffee ice cream, some of those crispy things...the French ones...the elephant things...Lizzie will know...and freshly squeezed orange juice. But it has to be very fresh. Tell her to pick a jug from the back and to check the date."

As Granny dictated, Tim scribbled furiously, and I mean furiously.

"Is that everything, ma'am?" Boss asked, just barely containing himself.

"Yes, that will do," Granny insisted, and clicked off.

"I'm so sorry, boss," I pleaded. "I'm so, so sorry. That was my mother's mother. She's a bit incognizant. I'll make sure she never calls again," I declared, knowing I could make sure of no such thing.

"Nonsense, Liz. I think that might have been the highlight of my week," he said. "Now I don't want to keep you from your work any longer, since I know how busy you are."

Derek tried unsuccessfully to stifle his snickering as O'Donnell headed back down the hall, and Tim slammed Granny's list on my desk before joining him.

"And to think this is only your first day," Derek taunted. "I think you finally won Tim over!"

* * *

Casey was leaning over the bar with her knees on one of the bar stools, laughing hysterically at whatever Brandon was saying. I watched them through the glass front doors for a second before entering. Something about nighttime at Millies always felt like a movie—probably because the dim orange lights can't help but make you romanticize everything. It felt like an escape.

"Well if it isn't the granddaughter of Ben Mason! *The District's* new hire! I can't believe she made time for us with that busy journalist schedule!" exclaimed Casey, stumbling out of the chair and hugging me.

"Shut up. Brandon, how much has she had?" I scolded.

"You think I can take people's orders, close out tabs, *and* keep track of how many times she reaches over the bar?"

I laughed. "Just don't light any candles—she smells flammable."

I sat down next to Casey and she told me all about the last few weeks. She had run off with the drummer of some Nashville band, and (shockingly) they were no longer together. She had a habit of throwing caution to the wind and following whatever guy was around at time. I didn't hold it against her because it meant she would always come home with the best stories.

"So, you like the job, kid?" asked Brandon, drying a mason jar with a putrid rag. *Note to self: only drink from Mason jars you've washed yourself.*

"I think so. Today was cool. Can I tell you a secret?" I asked, knowing Casey was too busy singing along to Jackson Browne to pay attention.

"Shoot," said Brandon.

"I'm covering the White House."

"No shit! Already? How the hell?"

"Well, I'm starting by writing a backgrounder on the new bill. But O'Donnell said it would be kind of a gateway into being *The District's* West Wing correspondent."

"Wow, Liz." He stopped drying the jar and smiled, "Listen, no matter how much we make fun of you here, we're proud of you. I sure am."

"Thanks, Brandon. I could never leave Millies, at least not anytime soon. I love you guys."

"Right back at you kid, but mostly because I won't be getting hired to cover the White House anytime soon," he chuckled and placed clean glasses on the shelf. No one could ever replace Mom. She was always the first person I wanted to tell everything to, and she was always so proud. No one could replace that. But my Millies family sure came close.

It was slightly past 9:30 p.m. when Christian came out from the back office to announce the kitchen leftovers were out.

"Chicken tenders, corn, steak...salad?" I asked Brandon, seeing how he couldn't leave the customers at the bar.

"Bingo," he nodded.

I shuffled my way into the crowd of servers and food runners all hunched over the kitchen island like a pack of ravenous wolves. Never get in the way of a restaurant employee and dinner—they likely haven't eaten in nine hours.

I made it back to bar with three to-go platters just in time to hear Casey bellowing at nearby customers,

"They're called breasts!" she exploded, slurring just enough to sound intoxicated. I froze. "I have two of them. As does every female in the species," she turned to face the entire bar area, "and, gentlemen, if you want to cop a feel or just stare freely at a pair of breasts without engaging with the person attached to them, there are women who get paid to provide such services. And they make a hell of a lot more than I do."

Her speech was met with silence, and Brandon stared at me with wide eyes and nodded at the front door, mouthing "time to go."

I practically threw his box of food on the counter and helped Casey out of her bar stool, clutching our food in my other hand. "Off we go!" I smiled sarcastically in Brandon's direction.

Just as we made it out of the front door, Casey burst out laughing, "Did you see their faces?" I couldn't help but chuckle as I put her in the passenger seat of my Jeep. "Like deer in headlights!" she continued.

"Yeah, Case, I'm sure they were quaking in their wingtips."

I closed the door gently and made my way around to the driver's seat. I couldn't humor her with my praise for such behavior, especially at our place of work, but it felt damn good to see Casey put those guys in their place.

I pulled out onto Massachusetts Avenue to head home, and the dim street lights made me realize how tired I was. Our house was on a leafy street in Spring Valley, only about three blocks away from Millies, so I usually walked unless it was rainy. It was an English Tudor painted gray, with black shutters and a long, unused stairway leading up to the front door. I always parked in the back driveway, where so many times I came home to find Mom sitting on the porch looking at the trees. It wasn't the largest house in the neighborhood, but also not the smallest.

When I pulled down our driveway and up to the back porch, I could smell her cigarette before even catching a glimpse of her dark hair and imposing figure.

"You could have told me you were in the big leagues so I didn't have to drive my ass all the way over here after reading it online!"

"Hi, Rhonda."

I smiled and fell into her arms like a rag doll. Rhonda was our everything person. She had known my mother for twenty years. She used to bring groceries to Granny after meeting her at CVS one time, and she eventually took on the task of making sure Eleanor Mason got out of bed every day during the divorce. Rhonda was the first person I called whenever I had a problem. I don't even remember meeting her, just that she had always been there.

Rhonda was a Catholic Italian from New Jersey—basically a tiger in human form. Her mom died when she was fifteen and she raised her little brother in a tiny town house with no heat. After twenty years putting up with my mother, and twenty years of my mother putting up with her, she was my guardian angel, helping keep Eleanor Mason's presence immortal.

"I see Casey is back." She crossed her arms as Casey pulled herself out of the car and up to the porch to meet us.

"Casey darling!" Rhonda bellowed, and Casey winced. "Honey, you look like you lost your lunch money."

I couldn't help but laugh as I unlocked the front door. "You can sleep with me in Mom's bed or in my room, I don't care," I said to Casey.

"I'll decide when I'm done puking," she mumbled as she headed inside.

I placed my bag on one of the Tucson patio chairs and reached my hand out for a hit of Rhonda's cigarette. The taste wouldn't leave my throat, even after brushing my teeth and eating. I can't describe why cigarettes are so good. I don't think anyone can. But you don't cry after a cigarette, it makes you feel invincible for five minutes, and without those five minutes you think you'd go insane.

"How was your day?" I asked after taking a puff. Rhonda never seemed to have a good day, but she was always in a good mood and with sound advice.

"I'm exhausted," she huffed as we found seats on the wooden porch stairs. "I want to meet a rich guy and live happily ever after."

I laughed, but not just at her comment. One day Rhonda would come in declaring she was done with men for good, and the next preaching about happily ever after.

"I thought the rich guys were all in Manhattan," I replied.

"The New York guys are all going after eighteen-year-old models fresh off the boat from Slovenia. There is plenty of cash here. Technology, health care, outsourcing…even war… my God, it's like money is just growing on those cherry blossom trees. It's the new gilded age in DC, honey. Anyway, conveniently there aren't a lot of modeling agencies here, so the bar is lower. Not a lot of cover girls looking to make it in a government town, gilded or not."

"Well, speaking from experience, people with power and money can be majorly screwed up."

"It's better to be screwed up in a pair of Manolos with a house in Aspen than wearing Nine West shoes and saving up for a week in Ocean City. Manolos are better than sex," she said, "and they last longer."

Rhonda stood up swiftly. "Alright honey, just needed to lay eyes on you. Gotta go make sure my brother hasn't burned the house down."

"Love you," I said, pulling myself up with the banister.

"Love you!" she squealed, and that was that.

Casey was, unsurprisingly, passed out with her shoes on in Mom's bed. I pulled off the faux leather biker boots, washed my face, and climbed in next to her. I hadn't thought about Mom all night, and even though she caused a scene, I was grateful to Casey for the reprieve.

CHAPTER

SIX

"Politics gets me out of bed in the morning."

—*STEPHANIE CUTTER*

If you aren't both willing and prepared to have at least one current events conversation per day, Washington is not the place for you.

I woke up on Thursday morning to the most news alerts I had seen on my phone screen since the election. After rubbing my eyes and blinking away the fatigue, I could just barely read the words:

"PRESIDENT SALINA APPOINTS DEMOCRAT SENATOR DAVID RICHARDS OF MARYLAND TO THE SECRETARY OF STATE, A NAME NOT SEEN ON MONDAY'S LEAKED LIST."

Shit. I thought. *Tim is definitely having a cow. He just wrote that Bonham would be the pick yesterday.* President Salina only had one other Democrat on his cabinet, but this wasn't just any cabinet member. This was the secretary of state. After reading a few articles, I learned Senator Richards had campaigned to be "a bridge between the two parties." The pick could make President Salina more likable, but it could also look like flip-flopping to the Republicans.

After tearing the covers off and rushing to the bathroom mirror, I dialed Derek on my cell. He had become somewhat of a friend over the last two days, and was much more familiar with Tim's breakdowns than I was.

"So, you've heard," he said ominously.

"Are you on your way to work yet?" I asked, cupping sink water to my face.

"Walking down the stairs now, you?"

"Just got out of bed. What are we walking into?" I patted my face dry and examined my puffy eyes in the mirror.

"Ever seen a grown man have a temper tantrum?" he chuckled.

I laughed and carefully applied a much-needed layer of concealer. "Yikes. Well, have fun with that. I'll be in soon."

"Press conference today," Derek replied, as if I could forget such an event. "Wear shoes you can stand in—for a while."

With that he hung up, and I threw the rest of my makeup in my purse to be done in the car. The only shoes in my closet that were both comfortable and nice enough were a pair of Mom's Chanel flats that hadn't seen the light of day in at least ten years.

When the elevator doors opened, the office was silent. *Not a good sign.* Making my way through the lobby, Wendy looked like she was holding back tears. She smiled at me, but her eyes screamed for help. I rounded the corner, trying not to make any noise, and that's when I heard Tim's voice coming from behind O'Donnell's door.

"The president of the free world doesn't just pull names out of his ass for this kind of thing! But the list came straight from the White House. Richards' name was not on it. Yesterday, I was the first to know everything; today, I'm a fraud."

Tim was rambling. It would be funny if it wasn't kind of sad. I almost felt bad for him. When I got to my cubicle, Derek was hunched forward with his eyes laser-focused on his computer. I placed my purse on my desk and continued to eavesdrop, assuming Derek already was.

"It's alright, Tim," O'Donnell eased.

"It's most definitely not alright. I'll go to the press conference today, and I'll get to the bottom of this."

"No, Tim, you won't. Elizabeth will. We're not going to take away this opportunity away from her because your source failed you."

With that, Tim marched out of O'Donnell's and down the hall, greeting me with a familiar scowl. I most certainly did not feel bad for him.

As Derek and I watched him prowl, I didn't see a single office door open down the long hallway—everyone was probably hiding. I had received my temporary press pass and wore a thin white blouse with one of Mom's suits. Even though the pass said clearly, "Elizabeth Mason, The District," I had a bad case of imposter syndrome.

Wendy had handed me a stack of papers on my way out of the office, and I had just enough time standing in line outside the briefing room doors to look them over. On top was a map of the James S. Brady Briefing Room seating chart. When you watch the briefings on TV, it looks like a bunch of anxious reporters are packed in like sardines. But the layout of the room was actually quite specific.

Organizations like CBS, CNN, Fox, and ABC always had the front row of seats for their White House correspondent—and I mean always. The seating chart only changed when correspondents didn't show up soon enough to save their seat, or smaller media companies overtook larger ones that month.

I had only ever been inside the briefing room once before, when Mom got one of her White House friends to give us a tour. I was barely tall enough to look over the podium, but I still remembered the glass windows with the cameras and lighting behind them, and the beautiful star-spangled carpet where the president stands.

After finding a spot to stand against the right wall, the crowd of reporters with much higher pay grades began to quiet down. It was twenty minutes after three and I was glad to find that, just like on TV, the president was always fashionably late. Two secret service agents opened the doors from the West Wing and from them entered President Mark Salina followed by Secretary of Defense Jerry Manning and two men I identified as army generals from their heavily decorated army green service uniforms.

"Good afternoon, everyone. Please, take your seats," announced the secretary. He wore a thin pair of glasses low on his nose as he scanned the sea of reporters. Everyone was sweating to hear about Richards' appointment, and I knew whatever Secretary Manning had to say would go in one ear and out the other.

Luckily, Wire had a recording option; Derek said it would transcribe for me. I pressed the bright red button and set my phone on the top of the manila folder.

"This week, the Department of Defense, along with members of the executive office and the United States military, have reviewed a bipartisan bill which aims to privatize and Americanize wartime supplies, in an effort to ensure our service men and women are provided with the highest quality of materials. I, along with my department and the president, believe this bill will further protect our military from foreign interference, and in turn will create a stronger American economy."

The crowd applauded Secretary Manning as he moved to the right for President Salina to take the podium. Cameras shuttered like crickets as the president nodded and said, "Thank you." I noticed he was much taller than I expected. His voice was smooth and not too deep. He had mostly gray hair which had once been dark blonde, and light eyes. He was too old to be Kennedy handsome, but he was what my mom would call a "silver fox."

"It is our duty to supply and protect our service men and women, who fight for our American freedoms every day, with all that they need," the president declared. "My support of this bill comes from my belief American goods are the best, and our American soldiers deserve the best. I hope members of both parties will make the right choice in getting this bill through Congress. I can promise you once it lands on my desk, it will become law."

The president spoke boldly as faces I had seen on TV were attentively listening in the front row, with a sea of smart-as-a-whip journalists behind them. Before I knew it, Secretary Manning had taken the podium once again and was describing in detail the language and specifics of the bill. I forced myself to refocus and caught the end of his address.

"This bill ensures at least 85 percent of wartime supplies come from American owned and based companies, with exceptions to extenuating circumstances. The president and I are confident the DUST Act will reestablish a stable and continuous supply of materials to our forces currently in the Middle East. Thank you."

With that, the president exited, followed by Manning and a wave of questions:

"Mr. President, can you comment on your choice of Senator Richards for secretary of state?"

"What happened to Greg Bonham?"

"Sir, the people deserve to know why you changed your mind!"

Press Secretary Stephanie Patten approached the podium to take questions as the wall of secret service agents escorted Secretary Manning and the president back into the heart of the West Wing. I had enough information for a solid backgrounder with my research from the days prior. *The bill is sure to pass in Congress, I thought. A military spending bill that focuses on making wartime contracts mostly American? It's a Republican's wet dream.*

"Good morning," Stephanie Patten announced. "Are there any questions about the DUST Act?" She scanned the room for raised hands, "Todd, yes."

A lanky man in a gray suit with dark hair lowered his hand, "Thank you, Madam Press Secretary," he fumbled with the microphone while standing up. "Secretary Manning explained wartime supply companies would be 85 percent American, with the exception of 'extenuating circumstances,'" he annunciated with air quotes. "What exactly would those circumstances entail?"

"Circumstances where we must attain resources from foreign entities," Patten said monotonously, "in the event of a major demand overseas for such resource or a shortage here in the US."

Todd nodded and took his seat.

"Nancy," Patten announced.

"Madam Press Secretary, I have here a quote from *The District's* recent article that Greg Bonham was in line for secretary of state. Why is that not the case?" asked a lady in the front row. As people began to sit down behind her, I could instantly tell by her signature dirty blonde blunt cut that it was Nancy Griffin from *Fox News.*

Press Secretary Patten sighed with irritation before regaining a composed tone, "The president never confirmed Senator Bonham was his choice. He was given a list of names and Richards is the one he chose."

"With all due respect, Ms. Patten," said Nancy, "it's clear Senator Bonham has more governing experience. We didn't even know Senator Richards was being vetted."

"Is that a question, Nancy?" asked Patten.

"My question is what's the story here?"

"The story is the president has chosen a smart, experienced man whom he believes to have the country's best interests at heart. That will be all, thank you." Stephanie closed a leather binder and exited the briefing room.

I felt my shoulders relax, until I noticed a familiar face in the corner of the room near the West Wing hallway doors. "It can't be," I whispered under my breath, turning the head of another freshman journalist to my left. It was Mr. Emerald Eyes, the green-eyed "recovering lawyer" from the other night at Millies. As I stared at him with a furrowed brow, he watched the press secretary carefully.

I leaned toward a woman in a green sweater standing next to me. She was respectfully smiling with her eyes, which made her seem nice.

"Who is that guy, over there?" I said, discretely pointing at Mr. Emerald Eyes.

"You must be new," she muttered, losing her nice façade. "That's Joseph Reilly. Do your homework. And shh!"

I knew before I even had to double-check that Joseph Reilly was the White House chief of staff. I had never caught his name at Millies.

I could barely focus on standing up straight, much less listen to the press corps' questions. When the briefing came to an end, I made my way over to where Mr. Joseph Reilly was standing. When he saw me, I could tell he was trying very hard to conceal a smile.

"I thought you said you were a lawyer?" I hissed, sounding just annoyed enough to hide my actual excitement over seeing him again.

"I said 'recovering lawyer.' So, I see the train writing worked out."

"Surprised?" I asked with a smirk. "Turns out I'm good for more than pouring tequila shots."

He laughed and leaned against the wall. "Well congratulations, Ms. Elizabeth Mason. What do you say we get a drink later? Someone else will be pouring the tequila, of course."

"In what world are you free enough for a drink during the week?" I asked. White House chiefs of staff barely have enough time to breathe.

"We don't exactly get off early for good behavior at the White House. Let's say 10 p.m."

He handed me a navy-blue ballpoint pen with "The White House" engraved in white. "I'm sure you know of a better place to get drinks around here than I do. Give me your number. I'll call you."

I wrote my number on the corner of one of Wendy's papers and tore it off. "Just call when the trains are running on time." I said, graciously stepping by him, barely hearing him chuckle, "so, when pigs fly."

The press corps enters and exits from the Northwest Gate, and as I made my way back out to the bustling world of Washington DC, I caught a strange comment from another reporter: "It shouldn't be hard. POTUS practically has Senator Morrison in his pocket."

Oklahoma Senator Michael Morrison was one of my grandfather's more conservative friends. Although they grew up only a few towns away, they didn't know each other until they both moved to Washington after college and their wives became friends. People don't realize how many political friendships transpire from their spouses' friendships. He had been coming over for dinner since I could remember, and GP insisted I call him "Uncle Mike."

Since I couldn't eavesdrop anymore without being too obvious, I made my way just close enough to see his name tag: Steven Bass, *Politico.*

The summer heat was making my face sweat like a pig, and after walking a few blocks, I hailed a taxi back to *The District.*

"Corner of Connecticut and Desales please!"

I dug through my purse to find my phone. Casey was going to freak.

Liz: "Remember the guy from Millies I told you about? Handsome. Bruce Springsteen."

She was quick to reply as I rolled down the window to feel the humid breeze on my face.

Casey: "Yes!"
Liz: "He's the president's chief of staff."

Casey: "Only in Washington."

"We're going on a date—10 p.m." I didn't really know if it was a date, but luckily Casey did.

"That's not a date. That's a drink. A date is dinner," she said.

"Chiefs of Staff don't have time for dinner," I argued.

"Try wearing something that wouldn't meet with your mom's approval."

I laughed out loud, causing an awkward moment of eye contact in the taxi driver's mirror. If my mother knew I was having a drink with the White House chief of staff, she would probably shove me out the door in five-inch stilettos.

When I returned to work, Wendy looked up with a bright-eyed smile. "How was it?" she asked, and I wondered if she wished she was more than a receptionist.

"Surreal," I said, in a tone that made me feel like I was back in high school, gossiping in the lunchroom. "In fact, once I finalize the backgrounder, I am getting a drink with Joe Reilly tonight."

Wendy cupped her hand against her mouth, attempting to hide a gasp, and then let out a harsh whisper, "White House Joe Reilly? Chief of Staff Reilly?"

"I guess so," I said. "He came into my restaurant the other night, but I didn't realize who he was until today."

I wasn't sure if I should be more nervous or more excited, when Wendy said, "Go home and change after work. The suit is beautiful, but not at all daring enough for a date with...," she teasingly looked around for any onlookers and whispered again, "Joe Reilly."

"Thank you, Wendy." I smiled and retreated back down the hallway to my desk. When I noticed Derek wasn't waiting to greet me with his familiar snarky comments, I pulled out my phone.

> Unknown (1)
> "If you're not too busy, I can meet you somewhere after work. Hopefully 10. You pick the place. Joe."

I knew exactly where to go. That is, if I could get the right person on the phone.

My mother had been bringing me to Cafe Milano since I could walk. They always added salmon to their "Insalata Milano" just for her, in classic Eleanor Mason fashion. Back then, she was simply Bennett Mason's daughter. After multiple occasions in which she had forgotten to fill my bottle with milk and asked the kitchen if they could assist, the *maître d'* introduced himself. His name was Leonardo, although he began going by Leonard when he moved to the States, and he called me baby girl. I dialed the restaurant on my cell and prayed Leonard was working.

"Cafe Milano," a deep female voice answered.

"Hi there! I was wondering if I could speak to Leonard?"

"May I have your name?" she asked, monotonously.

"Tell him it's Liz, Liz Mason...," I hesitated, but then decided I had no care for what this woman thought, "the baby girl."

"One moment please." The line went silent as I bit my nail. Maybe it was a stupid idea, but it's what Mom would have done. I considered hanging up right before Leonard's familiar Italian voice came through the speaker.

"Leeez, the baaaby girrl! How are you?" I couldn't help but let out a giggle.

"Leonard! I'm just fine. It's been a while." Years—it had been years. Mom had stopped wanting to be seen in places like Cafe Milano when she wasn't the glowing golden girl anymore, or at least didn't feel like it.

"It has been so long, my dear. My greatest condolences for your mother. We miss Eleanor dearly. She was such a dear friend."

"Thank you, Leonard. You always made her smile."

"And she made me laugh. What can I do for you... Miss Mason?"

"I am hoping to bring a friend in tonight, but he works in the White House. I'm not sure he would want to be trapped anywhere where people could bother him. Do you think you could save us a spot, maybe at the end of the bar? I hope it's not too much to ask."

"Of course baby girl. Anything for you—anything! We are family." I had successfully held back tears since my slip up at Starbucks, but Leonard was making it hard.

"Thank you, Leonard. Really. You are so kind. I will see you tonight."

"Yes, my dear," and with that he clicked off. And I started crying.

CHAPTER

SEVEN

"Turn your wounds into wisdom."

—*OPRAH WINFREY*

There is a place where politics, power, money, and fame are all equal currencies, where the famous-for-DC, the New York famous, and Hollywood celebrities can all find a seat at the table. It's called Cafe Milano.

It's the place to be seen in Washington. Sitting just off of Wisconsin Avenue in Georgetown, it was one of Mom's favorite places—perfect for any event from a ladies brunch to a Saturday night cocktail party. If Hollywood stars are testifying before Congress, they would usually be seen dining the night before at Milano. Sports stars, politicians, and Hollywood elite are all seen at the infamous corner table—hidden in the back room over whiskey and cigars, where many a presidential candidate have conspired with their closest advisors.

After I stepped out of the cab, I waited by the front door and pretended to be busy on my phone until Joe approached in a black town car. Watching the driver open his door, and him gracefully exit towards me, you would think we were at the Met Gala. He was glamorous but masculine at the same time.

"Well Ms. Mason, interesting choice for a drink," he said, motioning to a young woman in sky-high heels leaving with a much older man. Milano was exclusive and elegant, but not unfamiliar to escorts seeking business from successful older men who could park their Porsche and Maserati sports cars in the lot across the street.

"I'm surprised you haven't been here yet," I said, as we glided down the navy-blue carpeted stairs.

"There she eeeez. Baby girl!" said Leonard, gracefully sauntering out from behind the host desk.

"Hi Leonard, thank you again, so much," I said, as we greeted each other with the traditional cheek kisses. "This is my friend, Joe."

Leonard reached both hands out and grasped Joe's hand with one and his elbow with the other.

"Joseph Reilly, a pleasure to meet you, sir," Joe said sternly, with an infectiously handsome smile.

"Come, come," said Leonard, entering the bar area, "have a seat down at the end," he suggested, waving his right hand. I could already see two open spots at the very end of the bar. It was clear Leonard had pulled a few chairs, separating them from the rest. "You should have some privacy..." Leonard continued, placing his hands on our arms. It was in that moment I realized he reminded me of Lumière, the candelabra from *Beauty and the Beast*, except he isn't French.

"Lumi—ahem, Leonard, thank you so much. I am so grateful."

"Enjoy," Leonard said, smiling and retreating back to the front of the restaurant.

As Joe and I made our way to the seats, I wondered how to explain Leonard to him without launching right into a lot of family history. Luckily, the bartender approached us with napkins and waters. "Would you care for a drink, miss?"

I remembered I had told Joe I would only get one beer, but my speedy heart rate would simply not be eased with such a conservative order.

"Yes, please, whiskey with a couple rocks. Thank you."

"What on earth," Joe paused to take his jacket off, "would possess a girl like you to drink straight whiskey?"

I laughed and the bartender placed a short glass in front of me. After years of drinking vodka out of plastic bottles in college, whiskey made me feel grown up, even if I was only pretending.

"Whiskey's kinda like golf to me—I don't like it, but I keep trying to."

Joe laughed, and when the bartender returned with my short glass, he ordered a beer.

"So, miss-bartender-by-night-journalist-by-day, who was your very kind, very charismatic friend?"

"Leonard. I've been coming in here my entire life; he's like family. I didn't want anyone to bother you outside of work, so I called him earlier. You simply can't work in the White House and not know Leonard at Cafe Milano." I knew I was rambling, I just hoped Joe thought it was cute and not a side effect of nervousness.

"Well it's a good thing I met you," Joe smiled. "Someone has to tell me these things." *Say something, bimbo. He's just a dude.*

"That's what I'm here for," I blurted. *Jesus. Crickets, I hear crickets.*

"So aside from ordering whiskey straight and knowing everything about Washington," Joe continued, "tell me about yourself, Liz."

I had no idea where to begin. It had been a long time since anyone had asked me about myself.

"Well, you know I work at Millies…it's like home. And I just started at *The District*."

"Oh come on. I mean *yourself*, not your jobs." Joe was prodding, but I think I liked it.

"Alright Mr. Reilly, but you asked for it." I swirled the burgundy concoction before taking a generous swig. "I have an insane grandmother who calls my office in the middle of the day with her grocery lists, my mom recently passed away, and this was one of her favorite restaurants."

Joe's excited expression became somber. "Wow. I'm sorry to hear that Liz, what happened?"

"She got sick when I was a freshman in college—ovarian cancer. She hung on for a while but didn't want to do chemo anymore. It's okay. I'm okay. I let myself go, but now I'm back on my feet."

"Cheers to that," he said, smiling a warm and genuine smile before sipping his beer.

"And your dad?" he asked.

"Long story," I sighed.

"I have time."

"Haven't you learned when people say 'long story' they mean to stop prying?" I could feel the alcohol loosening up my tense shoulders and my heart rate decreasing.

"Sure, or they want you to ask about it."

He was right. It had been so long since I had talked about it I almost forgot how to.

"Well, I wish I could say he was an alcoholic, or died tragically. But the truth is he's just a narcissist. He wasn't very good to my mom when they were married, cheated on her. I guess when I got old enough to make my own decisions, it just didn't fly."

"What happened?" Joe asked. "I mean, if you don't mind me asking."

"I don't mind. It's just that it's a lot of baggage, you know?"

"People who don't have baggage are boring," Joe said, flashing his gorgeous green eyes in my direction. "I don't like boring."

It had been awhile since I had done anything close to flirting, but I was pretty sure this was it.

"Unfortunately, I'm anything but," Joe chuckled, and I took a sip of the watered-down whiskey. "Anyway, he did something to piss me off. I think I ignored him for about four days. He left me one voicemail, and never tried again. I was fifteen."

"What a dick," Joe blurted while shaking his head. Everyone I had ever confided in about my dad would say things like "time will heal things." Spoiler alert: it didn't.

"Right?" It felt like a weight had been lifted from my shoulders; I sat up a bit straighter.

Joe nodded sympathetically, seeming satisfied with my answer.

We sat in silence for a few moments before I couldn't help but hum along to Don Henley's "Dirty Laundry" playing through the bar speakers.

"What about you?" I finally asked, curious to know how he became the chief of staff at such a young age. "How did you end up where you are?"

"You mean in the White House?" he asked.

"Sure, in the White House, in DC, in this restaurant having a drink with me. All of that."

"Well, I grew up in Pittsburgh," he said as he took a sip. I felt a bit awkward having already known that from my prior Google search. Mom would have found his kindergarten teacher's name by now. "I went to undergrad at U Penn and law school outside of Boston."

"So, Harvard," I said confidently.

"How'd you know?" he asked.

"Anyone who says they went to school 'outside of Boston' either went to a school no one's ever heard of or doesn't want to say the H-word out loud."

"Yeah, well, it's just a name," he shrugged. "Sometimes I don't like the weight it carries."

"I can understand that. My grandfather was Bennett Mason."

"*The* Bennett Mason?" he asked with a wide-eyed expression. "My parents loved him."

"So did mine!" I said dramatically. Joe laughed and motioned to the bartender for another beer.

"A lot of people think I got my job just because of the name… Sometimes I do, too," I admitted, and realized it was the first time I'd ever told anyone.

"Well, those people are just jealous." I nodded and thought *that's what Mom always said.* Joe continued, "Even when connections get you somewhere, you need the substance and the character to back it up. I always tell myself that."

We sat in silence for a few moments. Something told me he was enjoying our conversation as much as I was, and I was dying to know more.

"Your parents must be so proud of you: Harvard to the White House."

Joe stared blankly at the countertop and scratched the beer bottle with his thumb nail.

"Joe?"

"They would be proud, if they were still here," he said softly.

"Oh. I'm so sorry, I didn't know."

"It's alright Liz, it's actually why I ended up where I am."

I sipped the last of my whiskey and waved at the bartender, showing him my empty glass. "How's that?"

"My dad was in the South Tower on 9/11, and my mom coped with booze and pills for some time until one day she didn't wake up." He trailed off for a moment, and I placed my hand on his arm,

"I'm so sorry. I'm so, so sorry Joe." I felt terrible, having just said I *wished* my father died tragically. He probably hated me now. I shook my head, "I shouldn't have said—"

"It's okay. Really," he reached over to squeeze my hand and continued. "When it happened, I spent almost a year just being angry—thinking she was selfish. I think she died knowing I was angry."

"No, she knew you loved her. Moms always do," I said, even though I wasn't so sure.

"I had just started college," he continued, "and I couldn't afford therapy, so I would go to the school's guidance counselor. Eventually she told me I could take the pain and use it. I should turn my anger into motivation. I wanted to get into public service— not politics—at first. So, I got my law degree, and went to work as counsel for a Pennsylvania senator on the Senate Judiciary Committee on Terrorism."

I wasn't sure what to say; it seemed as though he was happy to keep talking.

"When the election came around," he continued, "the president reached out to my former boss for advice on how to win Pennsylvania. I guess he saw an opportunity for the potential future president to be in debt to him, and practically turned our office into campaign headquarters. I was on the phone calling constituents for a week campaigning for Salina, and I have to believe it made a difference."

No one thought Salina would win Pennsylvania—it had generally gone to Democrats in the past few decades. I remember Mom saying Salina's win there was a "political miracle."

"It has to be kind of thrilling, no?" I asked. "Winning a swing state for the president?"

Joe looked intrigued as he spoke, "It certainly turned me on to politics." I caught myself once again looking into his indelible green eyes. "Anyway, Salina made the mistake of hiring one of his closest friends to be chief of staff, and it wasn't long before it became clear his friend didn't like playing second fiddle. I guess he asked around to find out who played the biggest role in the Pennsylvania win, and discovered me."

"The one who keeps the trains running on time," I smiled, and Joe did too.

"He asked that I move to DC, with the promise he would 'find a place' for me in the administration. It wasn't until I walked through the doors of the Oval Office I learned he meant chief of staff."

It was an incredible story, but something in Joe's expression seemed somber, and I realized even with all of his success, it was probably hard to feel happy without anyone to tell.

"I'm sure all you wanted to do was call your parents and tell them," I said.

"Yeah," he nodded and looked in my direction. "It's been hard to feel excited about it. I mean, I'm in a completely new town, and I haven't exactly made friends yet aside from a few staffers I know from the past. But now you can understand why I walked into your bar that night."

I laughed, "Well I'm glad you found Millies. It's a great place to make friends in this town. It's like my second home."

His phone began to buzz and when he looked down at it, a nervous look crossed his face. "I'm so sorry Liz, I gotta take this. Give me one second," he said, making his way to a quieter corner. As I sat there tapping my fingers on my glass, I realized I liked Joe. I liked him a lot. And it scared the hell out of me.

"I spoke to the president about Morrison yesterday. The appointment is definitely green-lighted, he just wants to wait for the right time, and he doesn't want to kick Manning to the curb." I wasn't trying to, but I found myself eavesdropping. Joe turned his back toward me and I couldn't hear the rest of the conversation.

Manning, I assumed, meant Jerry Manning, the current secretary of defense. I could only assume Morrison meant my Uncle Mike, and my entire body went cold. *The president was appointing Uncle Mike to secretary of defense. Is that why he would be in the president's pocket?*

Before I could finish my thought, Joe returned to his seat.

"Sorry. The trains, you know?"

I smiled, "Of course."

Then he looked at his watch and drained his glass. "Shall we go?" he asked.

Just like that, the magic was over.

Joe placed two twenties on the counter, more than enough to cover our drinks. Then he helped me out of the bar stool and we made our way back to the front door. There was a set of cement steps outside leading up to the street level. I was a little disoriented. Mostly from the whiskey.

Joe took hold of my arm to steady me, and then he kissed me. Gently and slowly, like it was happening in slow motion. He smelled good, and his chest felt warm as he wrapped his arms around me.

Then he took a step back and released me. I wondered if he would kiss me again. But then I realized I had some say in the matter as well.

"Can I drop you off someplace?" he said, pointing toward a black sedan idling at the curb. I could easily get a cab back home from the middle of Georgetown, but I didn't want the date to end.

"Only if this thing is bulletproof," I teased, and let him open the door for me. He closed it behind me and went around the other side, leaving me momentarily marooned. But as soon as he was inside the car, he reached for my hand. Then his lips once again found mine.

"You're amazing," he declared, coming up for air. It sounded nice to hear. But it also reminded me of the kind of thing men said when eager to get a woman's clothes off.

"What do you mean?" I asked.

"You've had to deal with a lot in life. Yet you seem so buoyant."

I tried but couldn't hold back a chuckle. "That's a first."

"I told you things tonight I don't think I've ever put into words before," he said. "You brought it out of me, Liz, and I have a feeling you do that for a lot of people."

I wasn't sure what to expect when we pulled up in front of my apartment. Would he kiss me goodnight? Would he tell the driver to wait and walk me to the door? Or more?

More. Much more. He dismissed the driver. We walked up the stairs of the back porch and it only took three tries for my key to find its way into the keyhole. As I turned on the lights, I prayed Casey hadn't left the kitchen a total mess. But then I remembered the dozens of boxes of Mom's things bound to distract from whatever remnants of food and dishes undoubtedly strewn about.

I don't think Joe was particularly interested in the tidiness of the house, or lack thereof. I found myself encircled by his arms, and felt the pleasant scratch of his stubble along my neck. It wasn't long before we settled onto the couch just after midnight and fell asleep in our clothes.

My mind couldn't help but drift back to Joe's phone call about Uncle Mike becoming secretary of defense. If anything shady was going on, talking to Steven Bass about his pocket-comment was my first step.

CHAPTER

EIGHT

"The job of a journalist is not to make anyone feel comfortable."

—SUSAN KING

It's easy to forget about sadness when you barely have enough time to breathe.

I almost didn't recognize my life since it had changed so much in the past few days. I was still in awe of the fact I had spent Thursday night at Cafe Milano and then on my living room couch with Joe Reilly. Then I remembered his phone call about my Uncle Mike. I shoved my face in my pillow and considered my options. *I could take it to O'Donnell, I thought. Mike Morrison is projected to be next secretary of defense. It's a hell of a story. But what if I'm wrong? Like Tim? Eavesdropping isn't always reliable. Then I fail and Joe hates me. Pass.*

I had woken up surprisingly energized for a Monday morning and decided to stop by Granny's before going to work. She lived just a few miles from Georgetown in a stately house she had lived in and refused to leave for thirty years. When Mom passed away, I stayed there for a while, but eventually it felt like I was just avoiding reality, a talent right out of Granny's handbook. Granny didn't have much left from her divorce payouts, likely from continuous stops at Saks and ordering dinner from The Palm, so the once charming brick colonial had fallen into disrepair. Fortunately, the trees and shrubbery were so overgrown the neighbors were mostly unaware of the eyesore.

As usual, Granny was stretched out on her living room chaise in a clingy nightgown with her yappy Yorkshire on her lap and her ever-present notepad in hand. Likely dictating a new list for me.

Granny had a tendency to see only what she wanted to see. It escaped her notice she was too old be painting black eyebrows on her face or that her little dog wasn't house trained and would squat and poop everywhere. Annoying as she was, I let her live in her fantasy land and tried to avoid stepping on the hardened little shits.

"Are you all right?" I asked, feeling guilty I hadn't come sooner.

"Oh, Lizzie, I had a terrible dream," she sobbed.

"I'm sorry, Granny," I said, relieved it wasn't something worse.

"I dreamt your mother was dead," she said hoarsely. "I woke up screaming, and I immediately called her. I called her cell phone. I called her home phone. But she didn't answer. I let it ring and ring, and Lizzie, she didn't answer."

Granny looked so forlorn and helpless, hunched over in her pink nightgown. I didn't know what to do. I couldn't decide if I should tell her the truth or make something up. But if I didn't tell her the truth, I would have to keep coming up with new explanations every time I saw her. How much better would it be for her to think her daughter was alive but refusing to talk to her?

"I'm so sorry," I finally said, sitting down beside her on the chaise. I put my hand on top of her small, birdlike one and caressed her paper-thin skin. "The reason Mom didn't answer her phone is that she's not there anymore. She passed away, Granny."

The crying stopped. She looked up at me with her cerulean blue eyes. When I was a child, they always reminded me of the ocean.

"I know Eleanor is dead," she said, "but I forgot." Her eyes clouded over. "Oh, Lizzie, I forgot."

* * *

I was so excited to put the backgrounder on O'Donnell's desk I almost tripped over my heels in the lobby.

"Good morning, Liz!" Wendy announced politely. I was still getting a read on her, but what I did notice was her constant nervousness over trying to please people. If she'd been at this job long enough, I'd suspect Tim was the cause, but because *The District* was so new it was more likely a childhood thing.

I collected the important information on the bill from the press conference and my research, and I even included a list of projections on how each senator would vote. The bill was likely to pass, having all fifty Republicans' votes and six projected from Democrats, of which included Senator David Richards. His Senate confirmation for secretary of state was scheduled to take place after the bill hearing.

Knocking lightly on O'Donnell's door, I gently opened it enough to stick my head through,

"Good morning, boss!"

"Liz! How'd it go?" he asked, swiveling around in his desk chair.

"You'll have to tell me," I said humbly, "it should have all the information we need."

"Right, yes. I'm sure the backgrounder is great," O'Donnell muttered. "I mean the press briefing! How was that?"

"Surreal, sir. I was close enough to see the president's wrinkles."

O'Donnell let out a marvelous belly laugh before turning to place the backgrounder on his desktop computer desk behind him. *Now or never, Liz.*

"Sir, I don't mean to overstep. I'm happy getting my feet wet. It's just, I might have a story—I need to get in touch with someone first. A source."

"Liz," O'Donnell said sternly, and I awaited admonishment. "I'm not sure what you're still doing here since there is a press briefing in forty-five minutes."

I lifted my chin, smiling, and forced myself not to shriek with excitement, "Really?"

"Your story is on the bill, correct?" he asked.

"Yes, sir." *Liar.* "Absolutely, thank you. I—I better go."

I turned to leave and already felt blood rushing to my head. *Your story is not on the bill, your story might not even be a story, and you have twenty-five minutes to get to the White House if you want to be let inside.*

I almost ran right into Tim in the hallway on my way out, but I was actually grateful to him for interrupting my thoughts.

"Watch it, Lyn!" he said, balancing his coffee mug in his right hand.

"For God's sake, it's Liz!" I barked.

O'Donnell groaned loudly from his office, "Play nice!"

"Sorry, busy," I muttered to Tim as he smiled a snarky grin and carried on down the hallway.

The White House was seven long blocks away, which I could manage in sneakers, and I was not going to succumb my bare feet to the germs of Connecticut Avenue. Hailing a cab in DC is not like hailing one in New York; you can't just stick your thumb in the air and hope for the best. It's more like being lucky enough to spy one coming down the street and then standing and waving so it is impossible for them not to see you. Which is exactly what I did.

When the cab pulled up near the Northwest Gate, I handed him a twenty-dollar bill and scooted out onto the pavement. Bartenders are never without cash. I kept my press badge zipped in a secret compartment of my purse, less for security reasons and more to avoid the crumbs of food undoubtedly swimming in the bottom of Mom's old Louis Vuitton.

Since the president and Secretary Manning had already addressed the bill in Thursday's briefing, it would likely just be Press Secretary Stephanie Patten answering questions today. The only question I had was for Steven Bass, and I thought about how I would approach him throughout the entire briefing. *"Hi Stephen, my name is Liz..." No. Get to the point. "Steven, buddy, what's your problem with Senator Morrison?" Okay, no, not a schoolyard bully.*

After playing with the words in my head and filing out of the briefing room, I knew what to say. And just in time.

"Steven! Hi." I held out my hand but he just stared, rightfully perplexed, and continued walking down the driveway from the West Wing. I followed, walking sideways to simultaneously face him.

"I was wondering what you meant when you said Senator Morrison is in the president's pocket? Liz Mason, *The District.*" That's when he stopped.

"*The District* has a White House correspondent?"

I nodded, "They do now. Anyway—"

"Yeah, I heard you," he snapped. "Did you flag me down just to ask me this?" he ask curiously as he motioned at the top of the driveway.

"Well, yes. Senator Morrison is a family friend. I was just concerned, that's all."

Steven lowered his shoulders, signaling his guard was down, "You could have Googled that," he said arrogantly. "POTUS helped Morrison become chairman of the Senate Defense Subcommittee back when he was in the Senate. Convinced other party members for him. Everyone knows that." *Everyone but me.* I looked at him with a pondering scowl, and he continued, "Guy's as old as dirt. Wouldn't want the president taking advantage of him from old favors, is all. It was just some playful gossip, tiger."

His smile made my skin crawl, and I watched Steven recede into bustling Pennsylvania Avenue with a school of photographers. I was both relieved Uncle Mike wasn't in any trouble and disappointed my lead didn't pan out. *Listen to you: your "lead?" Congratulations, you've met the Perez Hilton of the correspondent's club and you still don't have a story.*

After taking a deep breath, I turned left out of the gate onto Pennsylvania Avenue and began what would probably be my last walk to *The District.* That's when my phone buzzed.

Messages: (1) Unknown

"Nobody likes Steven Bass. Meet me in the downstairs bar of the Hay Adams in an hour. Have something that might interest you."

This day could not get any weirder. I looked around for hidden cameras and read the message again to make sure I wasn't dreaming. I very well could have been having a heat stroke. *Okay, Liz. Hay Adams Hotel, but who am I looking for? I typed a response after wiping the sweat from my forehead.*

"I'll be there. Who am I looking for?"

Meeting strangers in a bar is a great idea. Especially ones that also appear to be stalkers.

Unknown (1)
"Back corner, farthest booth from the entrance."

Just don't leave the sight of...anyone, I thought. The Hay Adams Hotel is directly across from the back of the White House; I would need to cross Pennsylvania Avenue into leafy Lafayette Square to get to this secret meeting. Since I no longer had the energy to worry about personal hygiene, I took my shoes off when I reached the park and carried them.

Something about being so close to the Mall reminded me of why I love this town. I knew so much about the architecture and the history, I guess it made me feel a bit closer to Mom and GP. Wearing her suit, I almost felt like a young Eleanor Mason. Except if she were me, she would never take off her Chanel flats and walk barefoot on the park sidewalk. I smiled as I imagined her telling me to brush my hair and keep my chin up.

Aside from a few side glances from other young professionals having lunch in the park, my shoe carrying didn't draw much attention. It was quarter to twelve, which meant I had about forty-five minutes to kill. I could see the hotel from where I was standing and lunged myself at the first park bench not occupied by a bum or a family of pigeons.

(1) Joe
"Missed you at WH today, dinner tonight?"

I had been so preoccupied with finding Steven Bass I hadn't even thought about seeing Joe at the White House. I honestly forgot he existed. But as I read the message over and over, my pigeon poop-induced scowl turned into a swooning smile. I felt like that little high school girl gawking at the quarterback again. I hadn't really talked to anyone the way I did with Joe the other night, and I definitely hadn't fallen asleep so happily next to anyone. It took me a minute to think of a reply, and I wondered if a message from me would make Joe smile like this.

"I know just the place, I'll call you when I get home. Maybe we make it farther than the couch this time?"

Since we had fallen asleep fully clothed on Thursday, and because he wasn't a pig, I wasn't entirely against sending Joe "the wrong message" as Granny would say. Having only ten minutes to get to the Hay Adams, I gathered my things and received a quicker response than I expected.

(1) Joe
"Is it me or did it just get really hot in here?"
"It's a date. Talk soon."

CHAPTER

NINE

"Washington DC is to lying what Wisconsin is to cheese."

—*DENNIS MILLER*

The few Washingtonians who just wanted a quiet drink without everyone in town knowing about it choose the Hay Adams bar, appropriately named Off the Record.

It's cozy but elegant, with rich burgundy walls, plush upholstered booths, and crystal chandeliers hanging from the pressed tin ceiling. It seemed to scream out "backroom deals are made here," and you could almost see the thick smoke that hung in the air prior to DC's smoking ban.

I made my way to the back corner, and to my surprise, the person behind the message was not the seedy-looking conspiracy theorist I expected. She looked to be in her thirties, wearing a low ponytail with a baseball cap and workout clothes. I approached the table and set my purse down, sliding into the booth.

"Hi, I'm Elizabeth Mason. I believe you messaged me?"

She looked up from one of the fancy menus, and I could barely keep in a gasp. It was Alicia Murray. She was counselor to the president until three months ago when she resigned due to an "unexpected pregnancy," per *People* magazine. My mother was obsessed with her always-chic outfits and never let me forget it, constantly saying things like "I found a tweed suit at Bloomingdales like the one Alicia Murray wore yesterday, you would look great if you dressed like her, Lizzie."

I suppose my surprise was obvious, as she quietly said, "I assume you know who I am, Liz?"

"Yes. Yes, ma'am, I do. My mother always talked about how fashionable you are." I tried not to be obvious as I examined her not-so-chic outfit. But looking like she was halfway into her pregnancy, I wouldn't care to look chic either.

"That's very sweet," she said cheerfully. "I know your mother. Well, I knew her. I'm very sorry for your loss" she placed her hand on mine for a brief moment. "She always had those magnificent media dinners."

We waited in an awkward silence, due to my utter shock, until she resumed,

"I guess I should explain how we got here." All I could muster was a nod. "Well, Liz, I have some information no one else has. It has taken me some time to figure out what to do with it. I'm sure you know Stephanie Patten?"

I nodded, "Yes ma'am, the press secretary."

"Liz, if we're going to continue this conversation, please call me Alicia. 'Ma'am' makes me feel like I'm fifty."

I smiled and nodded, "Okay."

"Stephanie and I have remained close since I left the West Wing, and when you first attended the press briefing last week she told me Bennett Mason's granddaughter was covering the White House. My parents loved your grandfather."

"Thank you ma—sorry, Alicia."

"Anyway," she went on, "I don't mean to sound like a stalker," *Please, stalk all you want,* "but I would like to think the granddaughter of a great reporter and a politically involved mother is equipped to handle what I have to say."

Whatever she was about to tell me, the goosebumps covering my entire body seemed to already know. , I thought, but Alicia was already ahead of me,

"Excuse me," she motioned to a nearby server with her left hand, "Can we get a—what would you like Liz? You're going to need one." She turned to me.

"I'll have an old fashioned." I quickly smiled at the waiter.

"Whiskey. That's bold of you."

I laughed, and she explained, "When I resigned a few months ago, it wasn't because of my pregnancy. I mean, I am pregnant, but that's not why I left."

By this time my anxious mind had come to the realization she was wearing these clothes to disguise herself. She didn't look anything like the woman my mother gawked over; she looked much more tired and casual—but that was the goal.

I listened attentively as the server placed a short glass in front of me. I couldn't help but bite the cherry off its stem, forgetting that young professional women don't do such a thing in meetings with secret messengers. *Is there an etiquette for this type of thing? Shut up, Liz. Pay attention.*

"A few weeks before I left, the president had a conversation with two senators which both surprised me and made me question my ability to accurately read body language."

Uncle Mike, I thought. *Oh no. Redemption for old favors.* "Was one of the senators Mike Morrison of Oklahoma?" I asked, swirling my ice with the plastic straw.

"That's correct, and the other is Senator David Richards of Maryland."

Richards had just been appointed as secretary of state, and I wondered whether to tell Alicia not only was Mike Morrison my "Uncle Mike," but I'd heard Joe's phone call about him.

"Anyway, when Stephanie told me your first task was to do a backgrounder on the DUST Act, I knew you were the one to hear this."

I went from twirling ice to practically drowning my drink. I stopped myself short of wondering where Joe stood in all of this in an effort to pay attention.

"I am only going to give you direct dialogue from this conversation. I don't want to infer anything. That's your job. I mean, you're the journalist, no?" I decided it appropriate to just nod whenever she asked these rhetorical questions. *Talk about etiquette.*

Alicia continued, "The president is sitting with these two senators, and essentially he says, 'I'm going to need a new team if we shift our foreign policy this aggressively. I'm going to need people like you to handle these things at State and Defense.'"

"Oh," I gasped, "well he already followed through with Richards."

"Morrison will likely be sometime soon," Alicia guessed. I bit my lip to avoid blurting out I had heard Joe's phone call. "When the president appointed Manning, he was getting ready to retire," she explained. "That's a known fact. It won't turn heads if he decides to replace him with Morrison, the chairman of the Senate *Defense* Subcommittee." I nodded. *Thanks to the president, per Steven Bass.*

"So he wanted the bill to get through," I said confidently, "and he's getting Richards and Morrison to whip votes in the

Senate from their parties in exchange for cabinet positions. That's Washington."

"Yes," she said. "Things like that happen all the time. My concern is the bill would most likely have passed without him doing this. It seemed...desperate," Alicia paused and nodded for a moment, "like he had something serious riding on it."

"The administration has been awfully quiet, except for the president's staff turnover. What's up with that?" I asked, a little more keen than I intended. But it seemed too eager of Alicia to quit just because of the meeting.

She squinted as though she had to remember her answer. "The president is a brilliant politician. It was clear from the moment he first became a senator. But his marriage always struck me the wrong way." Alicia paused, and I wasn't sure if she would go on.

"Regan is such a fabulous First Lady," I said, as I only really noticed her when her outfits occasionally graced the cover of *Vogue.*

"She is also smart as a whip," Alicia declared. "Her chief of staff used to say he'd like to see her in the Oval Office rather than the president. She was always itching to be a part of the action, and once people caught on to the fact she actually had good ideas, the president limited her access."

"How did she respond?"

"She thought he might be cheating on her. With me." Alicia looked up at me, her eyes were glossy and wet. "One day her chief of staff pulled me into the bathroom and told me what the First Lady had said, and instead of letting it become the gossip of the West Wing, I resigned. Blamed it on the pregnancy and said working would be too stressful."

"I'm so sorry, Alicia. That is awfully unfair."

"At least I'll be able to get a job after this," she huffed, gesturing to her baby bump. "I didn't leave with a cloud over my head." Alicia looked somber, but her eyes were no longer wet.

"Not at all," I said reassuringly, "just a lot of respect."

"So, look. Maybe this thing with the bill won't turn up anything, but I figure if there is something, you can get to the bottom of it while flying under the radar. I mean, no offense, but thanks to your pal Tim Marshall, *The District* doesn't exactly have a strong reputation."

Did she just say that? Oh, I wish I had that on video. For Wendy's sake. "Won't the president remember you were in the room and trace it back to you?" I asked. "I mean, if I find something I won't name my source, but I'll have to substantiate my reason for looking."

"If you gather up evidence of anything," Alicia lowered her voice, "he won't have any wiggle room to point fingers. It will be all damage control, and I doubt he remembers me placing a folder on his desk when this happened."

We sat there for a few moments in silence, and I thought about how much had changed in the last hour.

"What about Steven?" I asked. "How did you know I was with him."

"Lucky guess," she smirked. "Steven Bass is the gossip of the briefing room. I figured you would have run into him by now." She winked at me, and I couldn't tell if I was more scared or more turned on. Alicia looked more like an actress who plays the senior counselor than the actual senior counselor, even pregnant and in baggy sweats.

"Okay," I said, wondering what the hell I was supposed to do with secret information from Alicia fucking Murray.

Before my thoughts could completely spiral, she said sternly, "Liz, do whatever you can. This is Washington.

Conspiracies like this happen all the time. The difference here is you are the only one with this information. Some folks will tear you to shreds, and others are dying to see the government caught in fraud. You have to figure out which side you're on."

Alicia straightened her ball cap and placed twenty dollars on the counter. "Drink's on me, even though it's disgusting." She smiled that warm smile again, and I could barely get out the words, "I promise," before she was gone.

CHAPTER

TEN

"We are becoming the men we wanted to marry."

—*GLORIA STEINEM*

Even though I'd spent my whole life in this town, Alicia had shown me a side with which I was unfamiliar. I felt a little like Alice in *Through the Looking Glass*. Then I remembered what happened to her.

Sitting in the back of a cab with no air conditioning was not doing any good for my tension headache. It wasn't just the information that stressed me out. It was also the pressure of not wanting to let Alicia down.

When the cab dropped me off outside of *The District's* building on Connecticut Avenue, I didn't even bother going back into the office. I headed straight for my car in the parking lot and blasted the AC all the way home.

"Wendy, it's Liz," I muttered through the phone.

"Liz, hi! Is everything alright?" I didn't have time for her neuroticism.

"Yes. I was wondering if you could let O'Donnell know I am following up on a lead and won't be back in the office today."

"I can do that. I can do that for sure," she stuttered. "He will understand."

"Thank you, Wendy."

"Alright. Goodbye Liz!"

"Goodbye."

After fussing with Mom's increasingly difficult front door lock, I threw my purse on the counter and raced to get in the shower. I knew the feeling of harboring a dirty secret would wash down the drain along with the pigeon poop probably stuck to the bottoms of my feet. Casey always used to tease me for showering all the time, and I was glad she was on her shift at Millies. It just always felt like there was something I needed to wash out of my system or, more precisely, my brain.

Of course, I nicked my knee while shaving too quickly. I grabbed a wad of toilet paper and stuck it to my bloody knee, watching it immediately fall off. So, I found packaging tape, not in the medicine cabinet, but in a kitchen drawer. I wrapped it around the toilet paper on my knee, which made it look like I had just been in a major car accident—and was treated in a third-world hospital. But I had to keep moving. Hopefully the blood would stop gushing by the time I left for dinner.

When I finished drying my hair and doing a load of laundry, I decided to call Rhonda for advice.

"Hi honey!" she said, surprisingly not sounding busy. Rhonda was always busy.

"Rhonda, I'm freaking out," I huffed, putting her on speaker and anxiously folding laundry. Time flies when you feel guilty.

"What's going on? But first, breathe," she commanded.

I gathered myself and waited until I knew exactly how to explain it. "I had a meeting with a source today. A source no one else has. Something might be going on in the White House, and I'm not sure if Joe is involved. And we're getting dinner soon. I just don't know what to do."

"Oh please. You don't know what to do? Is the sky still blue?" Honestly, don't jinx it. "This is your career we're talking about," she continued. "Men come second."

So we're done with wanting to marry a rich one, I see. "I know, I know. But I really like him, I do, and I believe he's a good guy."

"From what? The two conversations you've had?" She laughed, and I was transported back to the days when I would call her with ridiculous teenage boy drama.

"My advice is this: keep at it, see what you can find out, and if you find you can really trust him, be honest. You are one of one. He is one of millions." That's debatable.

Of course, she couldn't understand completely, and I couldn't tell her what Alicia had told me, but she was still right. I owed it to myself to trust my gut.

"Okay. You're right," I agreed.

"Now, if you're getting dinner tonight, pour yourself a glass of wine and get ready! You might be in the workforce now but it doesn't mean you have to give up your life."

"I'm thinking the Capital Grille," I told her, hoping she would approve.

"Sexy!" I could hear the grin in her voice, "and the perfect DC dining spot! Tell him to order the steak! I gotta go, honey. Take a deep breath. Only good things!"

I smiled and did exactly what she told me to. All I had was a bottle of cheap chardonnay, but it would have to do. It also gave me just enough confidence to call Joe.

"Liz!" I had to bite my lip to stop myself from giggling at the sound of his voice. "How was work?"

"Oh, you know, just keeping the trains running on time," I gushed.

He laughed, and I could feel my heartbeat increase. "What are you thinking for tonight?"

"The Capital Grille. It's just around the corner from the White House on Pennsylvania Avenue, and I can meet you there around 7:30?"

"Works for me. I'll be coming straight from the White House, but I can probably make 7:30 work. I'll see you then."

"See you soon," I said, hanging up and beginning to get ready.

I opened Mom's closet, flummoxed as to what one wears to dinner with the White House chief of staff whilst possibly conspiring against the president. I decided on a black high-neck vintage Valentino dress which looked like a shorter version of what Holly Golightly wears in *Breakfast at Tiffany's*. Probably not what Audrey Hepburn would recommend for the occasion. Audrey Hepburn would probably recommend staying home and getting to work.

When my makeup was done and I had pulled on my last heel, I downed a generous five ounce pour of chardonnay and got on my merry way.

My cab pulled up to the red sandstone corner edifice a few minutes after 7:30 p.m., and I trotted to the front doors as fast as I could in my heels.

An older man was standing with Joe near the lion statues guarding the restaurant entrance, and I realized it was my Uncle Mike. Great.

"The president only chooses the best for his cabinet, Senator Morrison," said Joe, and I knew no one was supposed to hear that.

Uncle Mike patted Joe on the back and turned to leave. That's when he saw me.

"Lizzie Mason!" he called out, smiling broadly. "What are you doing here, pretty lady?"

"Uncle Mike, how are you?" I asked as I was engulfed in a big hug with Joe looking on, somewhat perplexed.

"Joe, have you met Lizzie—I mean, Liz Mason? Her grandfather and I go way back. Boy Lizzie, do you have his eyes!"

Joe didn't miss a beat before taking my hand in his. "As a matter of fact, I've already had the pleasure." His hand was warm, but his voice was professional as he asked, "How are you this evening?"

"I'm very fine. Thank you, Mr. Reilly." I'm sure Uncle Mike could see right through it, but it was childishly fun to pretend we were strictly professional acquaintances. Uncle Mike receded into a black town car as Joe and I headed inside,

"You know I wasn't going to mention it, but having Bennett Mason as your grandfather is quite the leg up in the journalism world, huh?" Joe asked.

You have no idea. "It certainly has its benefits."

We were taken to a table for two in the back corner of the historical-looking dining room.

"This week has been tough, Liz. Sometimes, I feel like an imposter."

"I can't even describe how well I understand that feeling," I admitted, checking to see if his expression became suspicious.

"Every morning I think the president's going to come into my office and say, 'Reilly, we've found you out. You don't belong here, clear out!'"

"That's ridiculous."

"Maybe so, but it's still how I feel." He took a sip of the Stella Artois he ordered. Just like he ordered at Millies. "In school, I was the scholarship student among the kids with the big houses and the fancy names. I always felt like I had to do twice as much to level the playing field. That never goes away."

I didn't really know what to say. I had always felt like everything was handed to me—hell, even my job. But I understood life wasn't fair. If it was, my mom would still be here.

"That's why you're the White House chief of staff and those kids from high school aren't, Joe. Shouldn't that make you feel like you earned it?"

"Some days it does. But some days I feel like it's too good to be true."

I nodded. Even though my investigation could take away my dream job and dream guy in a heartbeat, I tried to forget. For this dinner, I was just a girl, and he was just a guy.

When our server began to clear plates from the table, Joe leaned back and loosened his tie. "That might have been the second-best steak I've ever had."

"Not the first?" I asked.

"My mom could pan-sear a filet mignon like nobody's business," he replied with a warm smile.

"For my mom, it was burgers." I added, "She would marinate them in pickle juice!"

Joe leaned in close to me, "Should we take a walk?"

"Sure!" I exclaimed, "We can be tourists in our own city."

"I think I'm always a tourist. When is the statute of limitations up on that?" Joe asked.

"Hmmm," I pondered, "when you can drive from Rock Creek Park to Nationals Park without a map." Joe looked at me with fearfully wide eyes as we exited back out onto Pennsylvania Avenue.

I decided to take Joe up Ninth Street and then back down New York Avenue to reach the White House. After a few blocks, a brightly lit store window caught my eye. It was Tiffany's, the jewelry store known as much for its robin's-egg-blue boxes as for the precious items inside them. I stopped for a moment in front of the store to admire the display.

"Just goes to show very little can keep a woman from admiring jewelry," Joe teased.

"No," I replied, swatting his arm in mock reproach, "I'm not like that."

"Well, something got your attention, and it wasn't my devilishly handsome good looks reflected in the window."

"See those pearl earrings," I said, pointing to a pair near the front of the display window. "The ones with gold cuffs wrapped around them? My mom had a pair exactly like that when I was little. They were a gift from GP, I mean Bennett, when I was born."

"Did your mom leave them to you?" Joe asked, reaching his arm around me and squeezing my shoulder.

"I was too young. But sometimes my mom used to let me play dress up, and she would pull out the big wooden jewelry box she still has, I mean, she had," I corrected myself, "and I used to go through all the miniature drawers until I found those earrings. Then I would put them on and stand in front of the mirror, admiring the pearls. She told me they came from the sea, that they took years and years to grow inside of a shell, and they were God's way of teaching us beautiful things come with patience and faith."

"I guess they belong to you now," he assured me, gazing at the small white pearls.

"No, they disappeared years ago. Mom was convinced someone stole them. I don't know. But they were gone, and they were never replaced."

"She must have missed them."

"Well actually, she cherished the gesture more than the jewelry, but I loved the earrings."

We walked the last couple blocks in silence. Joe held my hand, and I found myself thinking about Mom and those long ago days of dress up and how happy I'd been.

"Unfortunately," Joe said as we once again climbed into a black SUV, "I have to sit in on an intelligence briefing at seven in the morning. It's not something I do every day, but tomorrow I have to."

"How come?" I asked. I immediately realized it was a really stupid question, but Joe didn't say, "that was a really stupid question," or, "if I answered you, I'd have to kill you." He just said, "You're not used to this—and I'm glad." Somehow, that made him even more irresistible.

"You must need to go home then," I said coolly.

"First of all, I get to work at zero dark thirty so no one will see me do the proverbial walk of shame across West Executive Drive. Second, I have more clothes at the office than at home. Workout...tux...my job throws me scheduling curve balls every now and then," he said with a grin,

"I'd rather use the travel time grabbing some sleep, at your place."

I looked at him with a satisfied smirk, "My place it is."

* * *

I woke up to a Starbucks cup sitting on the nightstand, and Joe having already left for work.

It made me remember I spent the afternoon we met crying in Starbucks over my dead mother, and I couldn't decide whether she would shudder at the thought of Joe sleeping over or, more likely, high-five me.

That was sweet, I thought, sipping the chai latte. But then I noticed there was also a little blue Tiffany's box and a small card.

Liz—
These can by no means replace your mom's,
but I hope they serve as a reminder of her strength,
which so clearly lives on in you.
Joe

My eyes welled up and my smile fell into a grateful pout. I opened the box to find the same pearl earrings that had stopped me in my tracks in front of Tiffany's. I understood why my mother always said the gesture was more important than the earrings because the note by itself would have been enough. Not to mention Joe had to wake up to get the earrings and bring them back here before Tiffany's even opened.

I dialed his cell expecting to leave a voicemail, but his familiar gentle voice came through the phone. "Good Morning."

"How did you do it?" I asked eagerly. It seemed the gesture had also overpowered my morning sleepy voice.

"I had a friend at the NSA turn off their security system for a few minutes. Like taking candy from a baby."

"Good one," I teased, "Seriously!"

"Diane, the VP of Tiffany's, is a good friend of the president's. I emailed her last night about these earrings my girlfriend obsessed over, and she had them open the store early for me."

"Joe, it is so sweet—," I shifted my gaze from the small velvet box in my hand to the mirror, "Did you just say—"

"Liz, there are some things that can't really be put into words," he interrupted. "It's just a mutual feeling...We both have been through some losses, leaving these empty places in our hearts. But mine has felt fuller since you came along. So, for lack of a better term, I want to be your guy. I want you to be my girl."

I blinked a few times, only making it easier to see my frizzy hair and morning skin, before gathering the poise to speak.

"I'll be your girl, Joe."

CHAPTER

ELEVEN

"It doesn't matter how old you are, or what you do in your life, you never stop needing your mom."

—KATE WINSLET

"Hi sweetie," Mom said in her soft and elegant voice,. "are you busy?" If I had known what she was going to say next, I would have found somewhere to sit.

"I just finished at the doctor's office. I think they found what's been causing all my pain." I heard her car door shut as I quietly listened for more. "They think it might be a tumor." The word never had any meaning to me before. But when I heard it through the phone's speaker, it felt like a tornado had heaved me into midair, and I couldn't get back down to the ground. "They don't know yet if it's malignant, but I'm sure it will be fine." Everything in my heart wanted to believe her, but I wasn't going to be so stupid. I did my best not to let her hear I was already crying and asked her exactly what the doctor said.

I must have been walking home from Millies because I found myself kneeling in a grassy area around the corner from our house. I flew to Boston that same night, where she was seeing a specialist in women's cancers. I knew she wasn't telling me everything because she didn't want me to worry. It turned out there were multiple tumors—a lot of them. When it was time for her to go into surgery, she told me she wasn't going anywhere.

She stroked the ends of my hair with her ever-perfect pink fingernails as I leaned over to hug her, and she said we would have each other for many more years. Suddenly, an image of us at my wedding unfolded in my head, followed by her hugging my daughter when I came home for Christmas. Then I was holding her hand while she lay in bed, and I was saying goodbye. It was decades later in my thoughts, but the mere picture of it broke my heart. I didn't think it would come so soon.

"Liz! I made eggs and bacon!" Casey called from the kitchen, and my vision was snapped out of the past and back to the bathroom mirror. I was holding Mom's hairbrush, which is probably what sent me back there.

"Coming!" I hollered back, knowing Casey cooking was less of a treat and more of a mess for me to clean up when I got home from work. When I entered the kitchen, I was surprised to find she had laid out plates of eggs and bacon, and there wasn't a mess at all.

"How ya feeling?" she asked, and I wondered if I looked sick.

"Fine, why? Do I look alright?"

"You look great! Look at those earrings!"

"They're from Joe. I think he just asked me to be his girlfriend."

"Oh my god!" Casey exclaimed, walking around the island to sit next to me. "Elizabeth Reilly has a nice ring to it," she laughed.

"Oh please. Don't get ahead of yourself." Casey served me eggs as I reached for the bacon. "Do you want coffee? Orange juice? I think there's some in the fridge." Something was absolutely wrong with her.

"Case. You're not at Millies yet. Drop the server voice."

"Sorry," she said, shaking her head. She held her hands awkwardly, like she was waiting for something to do.

"What?" I cried. "Seriously, am I pale or something?"

"No, no. Not at all." Casey shook her head apologetically, "I just. I know today must be hard for you." It took me a moment before I remembered.

"Mom's birthday," I droned, pushing eggs around my plate with a fork. With everything going on distracting me, I hadn't even thought about the impending calendar date.

"Yeah," Casey sighed, squeezing my shoulder. Today was going to be hard for me. If Casey hadn't reminded me, I would have realized at work. The company of Derek would not bode well. I had a feeling this morning's flashback wouldn't be the first.

"Weird," I finally said, as it was all my brain could offer. "I'm not sure what to do." By then I felt the lump in my throat piercing the nerve to cry. With all the practice I'd had throughout the years, you would think I'd be able to stop it. Casey leaned in to hold me and the wails spilled out, scattering around me like a chandelier that had finally smashed to the ground. I didn't know if any amount of time or practice would stop it.

* * *

I felt dazed being back at the office. Nothing felt natural. I had no routine to reclaim, and no friends there to confide in about the last few days. What I wanted to do was tell my mom about Joe. Well, not the sleepover part, but the rest of it. I wanted to show her the earrings, but that wasn't possible, and thinking about it was not helping me to brace myself for the day ahead.

"You look like shit," Derek commented as I plopped myself into my desk chair. He had no idea, and I couldn't possibly be mad at him. My emotional battery needed time to recharge after what had just occurred in the kitchen

"Thanks," I teased, "and good morning to you, too." *And you look like you've never touched a hairbrush.*

"Still hungover from dinner?" I turned to offer him a confused scowl. "You're on *Daily Mail.*"

"What?" I shrieked, having not checked my email for a Google alert that morning.

"When were you gonna tell us you're *dating Joe Reilly?*"

I took out my phone and opened my email. "Oh, god." I had no problem with my and Joe's names in the same sentence being plastered on the internet, but I wasn't sure he'd feel the same.

White House chief of staff and DC bachelor Joe Reilly was seen having an intimate dinner not too far from Executive Drive with journalist Liz Mason, granddaughter of Bennett Mason. Strictly Professional? Or...

"We actually only started dating this morning," I said to Derek, and he grunted. His friendly charm from my first day had suddenly turned to a bitter coldness, and I didn't blame him. I'd been handed the White House when I walked in the door of *The District*, and now Joe. *Speaking of Joe...*

"Ugh. Welcome to Washington. It would seem we're the talk of the town." I messaged him, hoping he wasn't already upset. I could only imagine what the president would say. *"Joe, you're dating a reporter? Are you nuts?"* That is, if the commander in chief cared.

"Liz! Good morning," said O'Donnell as he cheerfully approached my cubicle wall.

"Good morning, sir!"

"If you'd like to watch the Senate hearing in my office, a few other writers will be joining us." He turned to look at Derek, who most certainly did not want an invitation. "You as well Derek!" he chirped, before trotting back down the hallway.

"Pass," Derek mumbled through clenched teeth. Two other staff members passed our cubicles, followed by Tim bearing a furrowed brow and eyes which were glued to his watch. I checked the bottom corner of my desktop for the time. If anything in Washington ever happened on time, the hearing would begin in three minutes.

"Liz, glad you could join us," O'Donnell said as he motioned toward the leather couch. "Let's see if your voting predictions pan out."

"I'm confident, Sir." I found a seat on the couch closet to the TV and flipped to a blank page in an old notebook I found in one of Mom's desk drawers. I knew the bill was going to pass. I was more focused on the senators' reactions.

When the roll call vote concluded, there were fifty-five yeas and forty-five nays. Every Republican and five Democrats, one less than I had predicted. O'Donnell muted the TV and addressed the other reporters in the room. "Liz predicted it! Everyone, I would like you to meet Miss Liz Mason. I can confidently say she will be our new White House correspondent. Indefinitely."

I smiled humbly and thanked O'Donnell. The other reporters smiled nicely and followed each other of his office. They didn't seem rude, just like they had other things to worry about.

"I'm so grateful, sir. I know I keep saying that." In fact, I was almost waiting for when I could stop saying it. I just wanted to do my job and not feel so incredibly honored all the time. I wanted to feel like I deserved it.

"I have much faith in you yet," said O'Donnell. I shook his hand and headed back down the hall. That's when Rhonda called.

"I saw *Daily Mail*, you look fabulous!" Rhonda screeched through the phone. I scurried through the lobby and into the kitchen to avoid being seen.

"Thank you," I said, failing to avoid a smile, "it was amazing. We walked by Tiffany's afterward, and I saw these beautiful pearl earrings. Like the one's Mom wore. When I woke up in the morning, they were sitting on the bedside table in a little blue box. I couldn't believe it."

"Oh! You should have heard me screaming from where you are!" Rhonda shouted. "Where can I get a Joe Reilly?"

"There must be a factory somewhere because he simply can't be a human man."

"Well remember what I said. He is one of millions. Next thing you know you'll be fighting over those earrings in a divorce. Remember: if the ring is too small, say no. That's what I tried to tell your mother. We don't take those."

"What?" I laughed, "Slow down there. No one is getting married."

"I know. I know. Remember my friend Renee, from college?" I didn't want to be rude, but I honestly didn't remember, so I stayed silent. "You know! Emmett and Renee! She's married to the president's brother, but she says her husband is jealous, so they never come to DC." I would have remembered that.

"I'm sure you've told me about her," I confirmed, even though I wasn't.

"Well, whatever. We've gotten closer since she came to DC last month. She's more eccentric these days...anyway, she called me earlier because they're getting a divorce. Oh, but don't tell anyone I said that. It's very much on the down low. And she's completely hysterical because Emmett is trying to take everything away from her. She even said he was trying to get her wedding ring!"

"That's awful." I hated divorce. I hated talking about it. I made a promise to myself I would do everything I can to avoid one. They're so mechanical, and family court is never fair.

"I know! I mean, she was billed for a full hour by her lawyer because their equity shares in something called MNDA Corp is in her name! Whatever the hell that is. He claims it belongs to him. I always told her to never marry a man with a jealous side. Well, never marry a man, period." It was hard to hear Rhonda's rant through the phone, and I could tell she was both driving and smoking a cigarette with the windows down.

"Alright Rhonda, I'll never marry a man!" I said sarcastically, which caught the attention of Tim walking by. "I have to go, love you!" I hung up the phone and began walking back toward the lobby. But Tim had other plans, blocking my exit by standing in the doorway.

"Joe Reilly, huh?" he said, looking down on me both physically and metaphorically.

"It's very recent," I said, managing a fake smile.

"There should be a rule against the press...," Tim dragged out the hissing sound before saying, "mingling with White House staff. Seems like that could get messy." I wanted to punch him square in the nose, even though he was absolutely right.

"I don't let relationships get in the way of my job, whatever it is," I said calmly, although I'd never actually had a job a relationship could jeopardize. Tim slid out of the door frame and into the kitchen, allowing me to escape. He was a thirty-year-old bully, and I was naive enough to believe those only existed in high school.

I found myself relieved to be tucked away in the corner of my cubicle. I had no one to impress there, and Derek certainly wasn't paying any attention to me. I began making a to-do list for the week, which wasn't much more than researching the bill and making sure Granny had her groceries, when my phone buzzed.

> Joe (1)
> "If I were to be seen out on the town with anyone, I'm glad it's you. Don't sweat it."

CHAPTER

TWELVE

"True beauty is knowing who you are and what you want and never apologizing for it."

—*P!NK*

Casey insisted I stop by Millies at the end of her serving shift and invite Joe to meet us for drinks. A Wednesday night meant Brandon was bartending and Christian was managing. It was like Joe was meeting my family, but even more important.

"What's he drink?" asked Brandon once I found a seat at the bar.

"A Stella," I replied confidently, having noticed him order it previously.

"Of course," Brandon chuckled. I've never understood why beer choice is so significant to men.

Just as Brandon popped the cap off the bottle and set it on the counter, Joe came bounding in through the patio doorway.

"Here he is!" I said to Brandon, who was predictably drying a mason jar and watching Joe approach.

"Joe! This is Brandon. Brandon, Joe."

"Hey," said Brandon, reaching out his hand.

Joe shook it firmly and smiled. "So, you're the one who has to deal with her!" which worked on Brandon like a charm.

"Hey man, that's you," Brandon replied. That's when Joe turned to kiss me and took a seat.

"I have good news and bad news," he declared, "the bad news is we need to double date this Saturday."

"With whom," I asked, wondering what new friends Joe had made in the city.

"That's the good news. The other couple is the president and First Lady."

"No way!" I shrieked. I could feel heads turn in my direction. "Why? How?"

"The president invited us to join him at the Kennedy Center for the National Symphony Orchestra Opening Ball."

"I thought that was in the fall? Wait," that's not the most important question, "The president knows who I am?"

Joe chuckled, "He's been hounding me to meet you since our first date," he said, "and of course, Diane told him about the earrings." I supposed the president has a right to know where and with whom his chief of staff is at all times. If it was possible to feel both incredibly foolish and elated at the same time, I was doing it.

"And yes," Joe continued, "it's usually in the fall, so I'm told. But they're starting a few months early because of construction plans for the Kennedy Center later in the year."

I nodded, still processing Joe's earlier statements. That's when I saw Brandon pointing to the bar schedule. "Shit. I'm working, aren't I?" I hollered at him.

"That you are," he shrugged. "I had a feeling this day would come."

“Oh, knock it off,” I responded with a solemn face. Brandon had mentioned I would have trouble keeping both my job at Millies and working for *The District*.

“What’s up?” Joe asked, rubbing my shoulder with the back of his fingers.

“I’m scheduled on Saturday.”

“It’s alright kid, I’ll take it,” Brandon smiled proudly. “You can’t turn down the president. He could put you on the No Fly List or something.”

Joe and I laughed, and that’s when Casey threw her arms around us. “Well if it isn’t the famous Joseph Reilly.” Joe chuckled and turned to give Casey a hug, when I felt my phone buzz.

A.M. (1)
“You didn’t find it important to mention that you’re dating Joseph Reilly?”

Shit. I hadn’t even thought about Alicia. I’m sure she probably felt betrayed. I thought of what to say as I heard Joe and Casey laughing. “It’s nice to finally meet you,” Joe said warmly, and I typed a quick response.

“We’ve been dating for about 12 hours. I should have mentioned earlier. You can still trust me.”

Casey crawled into the seat on the other side of Joe, and started asking him about Area 51. Joe had a way of changing the subject to get Casey to talk about herself like I had never seen before. By the time the last customer had left the bar area, they were sharing stories about their first kiss. Casey ordered us a round of tequila shots, and by ordered I mean asked Brandon with puppy dog eyes, and Christian came out from the back office to join. But Christian only drank red wine.

"How's the other job going?" Christian asked, swirling his wine glass and awkwardly shifting his gaze between Joe and me.

"I like it, a lot," I nodded, "but you're not getting rid of me!"

"As much as I try to," he teased.

"Hey Liz, you ever thought about traveling for work?" Brandon asked. Casey and Christian started cackling. It was a well-established fact geography had never been my strong suit, and they were trying to embarrass me in front of Joe, of whom everything was a strong suit.

When I was eight, I was asked at a private school interview what countries bordered the United States. I replied with absolute certainty, "Canada and Africa," and then pulled a deck of cards out of my Hello Kitty purse and asked the admissions lady if she would care to play poker. GP played poker with all of his important friends, and he'd told me I was supposed to act grown up in the interview.

"What are the countries bordering the Red Sea?" Christian asked, like I was back at the grade school interview. I thought he was supposed to be grilling Joe, not me.

"Umm…let's see…," I stalled. "Egypt and Israel."

Joe seemed to be fiddling with something under the table. He tapped my leg and handed me a cocktail napkin with a note.

"Saudi Arabia," I said, glancing downward at the napkin, "Jordan, Sudan, Yemen," Joe's handwriting could use some work, "and Ethiopia," I finished triumphantly.

Joe laughed.

"What did I say wrong?" I asked.

"Let me see your cheat sheet," Christian said. I sheepishly handed it over.

"Joe wrote Eritrea, not Ethiopia. Which is a relief because I was worried your geography skills were contagious."

"Don't need 'em to bartend!" I yelped at Christian. He filled a mason jar with coke and turned to leave the bar. "Whatever dude."

When Casey returned from gathering her items in the back, we said goodbye to Brandon and headed outside to my Jeep. Joe had passed the Millies test, and it felt like I had somehow reconciled my two very different Washington worlds.

* * *

When I got out of the shower after work on Thursday, I heard an incessant knocking at the front door. I grabbed a towel and wrung my hair out over the sink, hoping it was someone I could greet in a towel.

As I approached the door, I let out a sigh of relief. "Did you forget your key?"

"Mrs. Joseph Reilly, can I have your autograph?!" Casey ignored my question, pushing past me and leaping up the stairway. The heat of summer came right in with her.

"Shut up and help me figure out what to wear," I said, following behind her.

"Okay, well bright colors are out of the question—unless we're talking sophisticated green or confident red."

"Really? I was thinking I would wear hot pink with a massively obnoxious bow," I said sarcastically. "Just look at the options, Case."

"Black is boring and white is juvenile...What about navy? Navy or red, definitely," she said, sliding through the hangers.

I knew Mom had a beautiful J. Mendel navy gown she wore to the Meridian Ball years ago. Before I could go looking for it, Casey let out a victorious, "A-ha! This is the one." It was exactly the gown I was thinking of—silk and mermaid style, with one shoulder strap and optimal coverage. It was perfect.

"That's what I was thinking," I said, taking the dress from her hands and holding it close. It still had Mom's perfume on it. She used to mix Prada Amber and something from Chanel. Unique to only her.

"Now shoes," Casey exclaimed, reminding me of the night when Mom and I picked my prom outfit. This was slightly more exciting.

"The dress is long enough to cover my feet, I just want to wear what's comfortable. These ones," I said, holding up a pair of suede pumps which were just under three inches and wouldn't leave me searching for somewhere to sit down all night. They were Mom's go-to for nights like these.

"Okay, we've got the outfit, good. Any jewelry?" Case asked.

"No, I don't want to be too much," I insisted. The only bling I ever wore was a simple gold necklace with the smallest "EM" you have ever seen.

"Okay, well you need this," Casey said, handing me a small gold clutch, "for your phone, keys, lipstick, and a cigarette, just in case." She laughed, and I set the ensemble carefully aside

"What are you looking at?" I hissed, noticing a grimacing look on Casey's face.

"You are gorgeous," Casey insisted. "Your hair, on the other hand, is not."

"My hair?"

"When's the last time you saw the inside of a salon?"

I didn't even know the answer to this question. Before Mom got sick, I regularly accompanied her to her salon in Georgetown, and even in college I would drive home if I needed a trim. George at the Four Seasons is the insider place in Washington for everyone from House Speaker Nancy Pelosi to *CBS's* Norah O'Donnell. Mom had been going since she was in high school, and when she didn't have the strength to go out anymore, George himself, the Turkish owner, would come to our house on Sundays to blow-dry her hair. The little indulgence boosted her spirits, and George made her laugh like only he could.

I could only imagine the kind of ordeal it would take to make me over—I was still outgrowing my blonde phase from school. Everyone in the South goes blonde, so I did too.

"It's only 5:30 p.m., who can you call?" Casey asked. Ignoring her, I dialed George's on my cell as Casey picked at the ends of my hair. As always, Rick, the salon's manager, answered the phone. No one else was allowed near the front desk computer screens with the personal schedules of most of DC's political and media elite.

"Rick, it's Liz," I said, pushing Casey's hand away. "I need to make an emergency appointment."

"Mizzz Mason…finally the lost soul with split ends and ratty nails returns to the nest," Rick said in a familiar teasing tone.

Laughing, I said, "I know, I know. It's not a pretty picture here. I need cut, color, blowout…"

"Okay. Hold please." Conversations with Rick were always interrupted several times by "hold please." I waited until he picked up again.

"I can put you in a week from Thursday at 3 p.m. for the works," Rick said.

"Rick, this is a specific emergency. I need to come in Saturday," I said.

"That's fine," he responded. "A week from Saturday at noon."

"No! I need this Saturday. I'm going to the National Symphony Orchestra Ball."

"This Saturday! Honey, you think you can just disappear for months on end and expect me to move Heaven and Earth to accommodate *you*?"

Rick was called the "benevolent dictator" in a magazine article about George's. For his friends and long-time clients, he would work miracles to fit you in at the last minute. For the rude or pretentious, the wait time for an appointment could be as long as six weeks. Or, more likely, never.

"Hold please," he said, and the click again.

I waited about a minute before he returned to the line. "Well, Ms. Elizabeth Mason, I have you down for four o'clock Saturday." A four o'clock appointment was going to leave very little time for making it to the Kennedy Center on time, but I could change at the salon. I was just grateful to Rick for squeezing me in. "I want you to know, Liz, I'm only doing this on behalf of those poor musicians who might get distracted from their performance by your trailer trash roots and bushy eyebrows."

"I love you Rick," I said, knowing his sarcastic comments were Rick's version of saying he loved me, too. When I hung up I noticed Rhonda had replied.

CHAPTER

THIRTEEN

"If I want to knock a story off the front page, I just change my hairstyle."

—*HILLARY CLINTON*

When I walked in the front door of the salon, Rick came bounding out from behind the white, circular reception desk to greet me. He grabbed the garment bag I was trying to keep from dragging across the floor as we hugged and told me how much he missed my mom. Several other staff members joined in with heartfelt condolences, including George, who came over with tears in his eyes. It was completely out of character for the macho Turkish man, but I'd practically grown up in this salon, so we were like family.

Trying to lighten the mood, Rick said, "Remember the first time you came in on your own?"

My eyes were wet, but I laughed knowing what was coming next. "Rick! I was fifteen, don't I get a statute of limitation on this story?"

"Oh, I remember this!" said Servat, my stylist and George's youngest son. He had been doing my hair since I was five, and I blamed him for the bangs.

"Well, Liz was about to start tenth grade," Rick recalled, "and she had a store-bought box of blue hair dye in her hand, and a chunk of hair which was two shades away from being bleached right off!"

Laughing, Servat said, "I called it her self-inflicted wound."

Rick continued, "She begged us to fix it for her, and I did not want to be the man between Eleanor Mason and this rebellious young lady."

"She wouldn't have gotten mad at *you,*" I said softly as Servat handed me a robe.

"While she got shampooed," Rick continued, "I called her mother." My face began to feel hot from the tiny bit of teenage angst I still had left.

"So, Eleanor Mason hightails it over, with nary a hair out of place, and she says to Liz, 'What a delightfully fun and fleeting idea for you to have a hair color that screams unemployed.' Meanwhile Liz is fifteen, and Eleanor goes, 'I hope you've saved up enough money for it—that is not going on my credit card!'" Rick laughed as he retold the old story.

"So, Liz stormed out the door and sat on the curb in front smoking a cigarette. But Mrs. Mason didn't even notice. She came up to me and said calmly, 'Rick darling, is there an opening for a manicure? I chipped my polish rushing over here.' So, while Mrs. Mason was having her nails done, Liz came back inside and Little Miss Rebel Yell sat for a blow out and Servat dyed *everything* back to her natural brown."

Rick winked at me and I walked over with Servat to begin a much-needed transformation. I still had no idea what I was going to say to the president or first lady. I was wondering if

I could convince Joe to tell them I had laryngitis—or I was mute. Sitting in a salon gave me too much time to think, and thinking was dangerous.

I was only diverted from such deconstructive thoughts when I overheard a woman on the other side of the hairdresser's station. "Reilly, like O'Reilly on *Fox*, but without the 'O' and decades younger. He's the White House chief of staff, and he is gorgeous." I leaned forward and listened more. "Bob loves working with him, but I think Bob's also a little jealous because it seems...," the woman lowered her voice so much I had to practically put my ear to the mirror to hear, "...he's the only one the president trusts completely."

My worry Joe could be involved in shady doings with the president came knocking at my conscience's door while Servat pulled me back in my chair. But by then the woman's voice had returned to a normal register.

"I've been asking Bob to bring Joe Reilly to dinner to meet our middle daughter, Alexa. The one in med school at Georgetown. Of course, it's not going to happen this week because she's still at her modeling shoot in Milan. But wouldn't they be the perfect match?"

My Joe? Had she not seen *Daily Mail*? I realized I was clenching my jaw to the point of soreness and would have to alert this woman of Joe's relationship status before I exploded. But I was no competition for the supermodel-slash-surgeon she claimed her daughter to be. Servat stepped away to get more hair dye, and I dashed—awkwardly, holding my head steady—across the salon to Rick at the front desk.

"Rick," I said somewhat breathlessly. "Who's the woman on the other side of Ismail's station? She's talking about my boyfriend like he's single, and available, and perfect for her model-slash-doctor daughter."

"Listen tulip, calm down," Rick said soothingly. "Why on earth do you think she's talking about your guy?"

"Because she said so." I leaned in and whispered, "I'm dating Joe Reilly. Clearly she hasn't seen *Daily Mail*, and neither have you!"

Rick put his hand over his mouth, and his eyes widened. "You're going with *Joe Reilly* to the Honors?" I nodded. "Oh, honey, he's a beautiful man. Are you sure he's straight?"

"Yes. He's straight and maybe not immune to the charm of a swimsuit model who's going to be able to perform brain surgery. What should I do?"

"You should get back in your chair and let Servat finish your color before your hair turns orange. Leave the rest to me."

That really didn't seem like much of a plan, but I didn't have any better ideas. I sat back down while Servat tapped his foot impatiently.

No sooner was I in the seat, then Rick strutted to the center of the room. "Liz Mason!" he called out, "Joe Reilly is on line one! He says he has to talk to you before the cabinet meeting about tonight, and you're not answering your cell." God I loved Rick. If he could produce sheer ingenuity in such a short time, I could only imagine what plotted revenge would look like.

"Tell him I'll text him back. Thank you!" I shouted loudly enough to turn heads without being obvious.

The urge to look around the partition to see the woman's reaction was like an itch on the tip of my nose. I squinted into the mirror in hopes of avoiding a sneeze when I felt a tap on my shoulder. Servat released the paintbrush of hair dye from my scalp so I could look up,

"Excuse me," said a middle-aged blonde with perfectly stiff, blown-out hair. "Who are you?" she demanded without even bothering to introduce herself.

"Elizabeth Mason. How do you do?" I said in my most charming, confident voice.

"I heard Rick say you know Joe Reilly. Is that true?" She was challenging me, which just riled me up more.

"Yes ma'am, I do. Joe is my boyfriend. Do you know him?"

I could sense her irritation as her smile slowly dropped. "Well, yes, I know him. He works with my husband, Bob Schiff."

Bob Schiff was director of the National Economic Council, but I didn't have to let on I knew that.

"Oh, how lovely! I'll tell Joe we met."

"Darling, my husband has a very high-level job at the White House and has had one under several presidents," Mrs. Schiff bristled.

"I see. Then perhaps he knew my grandfather, Bennett Mason?" Take that, lady. This is not New York, like Rhonda said. In Washington, Mason heritage definitely trumps models, even if they're going to medical school.

"Bennett Mason?" she uneasily asked. "Oh, why yes. I knew him as well. I mean, not personally. But I understand he was a lovely man," she said with an obsequious smile, before slinking back toward her pedicure chair, saying, "nice to meet you, Elizabeth."

"You too," I said, with the most plastic smile I could muster.

If Mom were here, I thought, she would have done exactly the same thing. Except most women in Washington would be too nervous to approach Eleanor Mason.

It seemed only minutes later Servat swiveled the chair around with a dramatic flourish. "Our girl is back." he declared.

I stared at the person in the mirror like a stranger. There were bright honey highlights around my face and woven through my caramel-colored strands. I stood up and swung my soft, wavy mane around like a shampoo model. "Thank you, thank you, thank you!" I said, hugging him.

He laughed, "Oh if only you were always this excited about highlights and a blowout." He escorted me to Carl's corner of the salon, where pots of makeup were arrayed like treats at Dylan's Candy Bar. Carl didn't have a mirror at his table because he didn't want women complaining the whole time about their lines or their thin lips, but also because he liked the dramatic unveiling at the end of his artistry. So I sat, staring at Carl, praying he could work a miracle.

"Smile, *smile*!" Carl ordered, applying blush on my cheekbones. "Look down. Stop blinking. Just stare at my rock-hard abs," he said, while curling my lashes with a silver metal contraption. It took everything I had not to burst out laughing.

After forty-five minutes of being attentively serviced, Carl stood back and said "Perfect. Just perfect. You look fabulous, honey. Absolutely fabulous." He held up a hand mirror for me to see the results.

"Wow, Carl, who is that person?" I asked, shocked by how different I looked. Gone were the bags creeping up under my eyes and the pesky dark spots from before I learned you shouldn't pop zits. I actually looked like I had cheek bones. Carl had contoured my face into one from a magazine.

"It's the most gorgeous girl in Washington who's going on a date with the hottest bachelor in town," Carl said, smiling broadly. News traveled fast at George's.

Rick snuck up behind me, carrying my garment bag with the gown and shoes. "You look disgusting, absolutely disgusting!" he teased, whipping the garment bag around his shoulder.

I leaned in to kiss Rick on the cheek, but he recoiled, "The lips, honey! The lips! Air kisses only until the end of the night!" I knew that advice would wouldn't last long.

Carl pulled out tubes of lipstick and gloss. "Keep these for retouches if you absolutely must touch a glass or fork to your lips during dinner."

"A glass, or a fork, or your man!" teased Carl.

I nodded, feeling a little less sure of myself.

"And whatever you do," Carl added, "don't sweat."

* * *

I gracefully stepped into the cab, one heel bearing foot after the other, praying the humidity wouldn't dull my fresh blowout.

"Kennedy Center, please." I requested to the back of the driver's head.

"Traffic," he blurted, "I have to go around." If there's one thing I had learned from rush hour in the nation's capital, it's that you must memorize multiple routes to get somewhere.

Instead of taking Pennsylvania Avenue, the driver went back up M Street, through Georgetown, and zipped onto the Whitehurst Freeway. It was without a doubt my favorite road in the city. The buzzing freeway sits parallel to the Potomac River, and above K Street, curving through the Georgetown waterfront buildings. It had been awhile since I was in a passenger seat and could gaze out the window. As the taxi rounded the corner onto the elevated roadway, I could see the sun reflecting off the Arlington skyscrapers across the river. With the water almost perfectly still, the melted golden sunshine formed a glistening reflection on the river surface. Somehow, in the middle of a Washington DC freeway on a Saturday evening, everything seemed quiet.

For a brief moment before the freeway ends, you can see the Washington Monument poking out from behind the Watergate Hotel, and the Kennedy Center there next to it. Seeing the history of three presidents in one view, it feels like power of Washington might just rub off on you.

CHAPTER

FOURTEEN

"Rock and roll might not solve all your problems, but it does let you dance all over them."

—*PETE TOWNSHEND*

My taxi pulled into the Kennedy Center driveway at 6:50 p.m.—five minutes after I was supposed to be inside meeting Joe. There was a long line of taxis and limos in front of us, and I knew all too well how Washingtonians made slow entrances by stopping to talk to people and, even more importantly, making sure to be seen talking to people. I had no time; I paid the driver and zipped out of the cab.

My heels clacked on the concrete as I strode quickly toward the entrance. The heavy glass door silently swung shut behind me, and I was in the Hall of States, a long, red-carpeted hallway. Though "hallway" was an understatement—it was five stories high and nearly the length of a football field. It was also chock full of Washington's power brokers, everyone from senators to news reporters to top lobbyists. I was probably one of the few people there who wouldn't be recognized from photos in *The Washington Post.*

I took a deep breath, pulled my shoulders back, and forged ahead. There was a long table a few feet away where I was asked for my name and ID. My heart beat quickly as a well-coiffed redhead frowned while scanning a sheaf of papers. *What if my name wasn't there? Maybe I should have used Joe's name.* But I clearly wasn't the president's chief of staff.

"Right this way," the woman said, motioning me down the hall. Then she added, "I hope you and Mr. Reilly enjoy your evening."

It was really happening. I was at the Kennedy Center, and I was going to meet the president on the arm of Joe Reilly. I loved Joe, and I felt the full force of this sudden realization. I smiled inwardly, feeling the confidence of my freshly highlighted hair and decorated face. But then I remembered Alicia, and the DUST Act, and I hated myself for half a second. *What would Rhonda say?*

She'd likely tell me "I still deserve a life." So I lifted my head and kept going.

I continued to the grand foyer, which was more than twice the length of the Hall of States, with sixteen story-high crystal chandeliers dangling like elaborate earrings from the modernist white ceiling. I noticed a number of heads swivel as I walked by, and I was amused to see people trying to figure out who I was. But there was only one person who was of any interest to me.

There, at the far end of the room, I spotted the back of Joe's head. He was by the window, watching the sunset over the Potomac. Like a lot of powerful DC people, Joe preferred to stand in a corner with his back to the room, so he didn't get interrupted by lobbyists and job seekers.

Maybe it was my imagination, but it felt like the sea of bodies was parting for me as I floated through the elegant crowd. I tapped Joe on the shoulder, and when he turned around I nearly gasped. He looked magnificent in his tuxedo; he was easily the handsomest man I'd ever seen. He just stood there, staring at me.

"What's wrong?" I asked. *Was my dress too tight? Too revealing? Was I too made up?*

His face softened as he spoke with an intensity I'd never heard from him before. "Don't break my heart, Lizzie."

I laughed and shook my head. "Never."

"Shall we?" he asked, taking my arm as he led me to a security magnetometer. I had to hand over my metallic purse to the attendant for a physical inspection. Then arm-in-arm we ascended a long flight of circular steps with brass banisters to the box tier.

At the top, Joe handed our tickets to an usher, and I noted with some disappointment she was completely unimpressed. She simply nodded in the direction of the president's box, as if going there was an everyday occurrence. *Of course, I guess for her it was.*

It was obvious which box it was, since there was a presidential seal painted above the door, and a secret service agent stationed outside. He shook Joe's hand and opened the door for us, revealing a small lounge. There were gold-brocaded armchairs and upholstered benches, and the omnipresent Chinese red carpet.

"I'm going to run to the ladies room before it's rude to leave," I said, lifting the bottom of my dress so as to not trip over myself—although there were plenty of capable secret service men ready to pick me right back up if I did.

After floating through the dimly lit hallways of the suite for a few minutes, searching for any sign of a restroom, I found myself quite turned around. The layout of the suite resembled that of a cruise ship, but instead of sea sickness I had a bad case of imposter syndrome.

I had swallowed my pride and was ready to approach a secret service agent for directions, who looked much more akin to a statue than a human, when I saw a small staircase with a restroom sign. I wasn't sure if it was the myriad of perfumes in the air or the fact I hadn't really eaten dinner, but I felt lightheaded. I wondered if Alicia knew I was here. If she didn't already, she would by the time tomorrow's headlines hit the stands.

When I made it to the ladies' lounge, there was a room with a beautiful chandelier above plush, pale couches. It looked like the bathrooms you see in high-end Manhattan department stores. I was using the baking-flour-like foundation powder Carl gave me to blot the oil from my nose and forehead when I heard a woman's voice approaching from around the corner. I slid into one of the stalls in an attempt to avoid conversation.

"I can't imagine how hard it must be. Mark and I are here to support you in any way we can." *Mark as in Mark Salina? The president?* I wondered.

"Thank you, Regan," said the other woman, and the skin on my neck prickled when I realized it *was* the First Lady. I turned to round the corner as casually and quickly as I could, while still being close enough to hear.

The first woman continued, "Emmett has been fighting me so hard with the lawyers, but I just want to remain comfortable when this is all over." She sounded, for lack of a better word, heartbroken. I remembered Rhonda telling me about Emmett and Renee Salina's divorce.

"My advice, Renee: just let him have what he wants." The First Lady lowered her voice. "We want to keep this quiet. We can't run the of risk anyone finding out about Tommy."

It was too late for me to get back to Joe without them seeing me, so I pulled out my phone. "Okay, Granny, I heard you. I will come over first thing in the morning." I prayed they hadn't noticed me and concluded my fake phone call, "Okay. Yes. I love you too, Granny"

When I turned to make my way back to the balcony, the First Lady and Regan Salina were already ahead of me. I had successfully become invisible. *Who was Tommy? And why did they need to keep quiet?*

The search results for "Tommy Salina" were inconclusive, and I felt silly for thinking it would be so easy. Searching "Emmett and Renee Salina" brought me to the president's brother's Wikipedia page, and under the section of children I read the name Thomas Hall. After some high-school-level stalking, I figured out Hall was Renee's maiden name. *Why wouldn't he go by Salina?* There wasn't much else except an article saying he was volunteering in Belize with the Peace Corps.

I turned my phone back off and placed it inside my metallic clutch. I wished for a moment Joe had any other job in the world, so I wouldn't feel such guilt.

After retracing my steps back up the stairs and through security, I found myself beside Joe inside the presidential suite—not as an investigative journalist, but simply as Joe's girlfriend.

The door popped open, and the agent poked his head in. "POTUS inbound," he said to Joe before disappearing again. The door made a whooshing sound as it closed behind him.

"The doors are sound-proofed and airtight," Joe explained. Hearing the word made my breathing tense up. I wanted to run my fingers along Joe's dimples, but I resisted the impulse given the commander in chief was about to make an appearance. I wondered what the proper etiquette was for meeting the president. I had thus far expected to only do so on the other side of the briefing room, holding a microphone.

Curtsying seemed inappropriate. Yet it seemed somehow wrong to just smile and say hello, which was precisely what I did as the president burst into the room with the energy of a high school quarterback, introducing himself and the First Lady with a slight Texan drawl. He was even taller than I'd realized. But I recognized the striking light eyes and silver hair I'd seen from afar only a few weeks ago.

"Liz, I'm so happy to finally meet you," the president said, clasping my hand in both of his. He said it like he meant it, which was flattering and a little flustering. *What had Joe told him about me which would have earned such enthusiasm?*

"Now I'm willing to forgive you working for *The District* if you forgive my snoring during the Rachmaninoff."

The First Lady playfully swatted his arm. "There is no Rachmaninoff, and if you dare nod off, I give Liz permission to kick you in the shins." I didn't want to like her, for Alicia's sake, but she was much merrier than I expected.

"Are you a classical music fan, Liz?" President Salina asked. Again, he locked his eyes on mine, making me feel like there was nothing in the world more important for him than my taste in music. It was no accident he had sky-high approval ratings.

"My mother has been taking me to the National Symphony Orchestra since I was a girl," I said, "and I've always found it an excellent place for a nap."

The president let loose a deep, resonant laugh. I had never been in the presence of someone who exuded such extraordinary charisma. Not that Joe was lacking, but this was different—it was like a magnetic force field. Though it was currently aimed in my direction, I knew I was not the catalyst for his megawatt smile. Still, I felt myself swooning a little.

The lights flickered, and for a moment I thought the power of the president's personality was somehow impacting the electrical grid. In actuality, the lights were signaling the start of the performance. The president ushered everyone through another door. As Joe took my hand, I saw he was beaming, and so was I.

The president's box was in the center of a horseshoe-shaped ring of about twenty crimson-red boxes suspended around the proscenium. There were eight plush red seats arranged in two rows. I noticed Emmett and Renee Salina were sitting in the far-right corner. Her legs were crossed away from him as she sat staring at the stage like a statue. I knew what it was like, to pretend you aren't hurting. Her husband was leaving her, and because he happened to be the president's brother and because of someone named Tommy, she had to keep quiet.

The First Lady took a seat in the front row on the right. I didn't like the way she spoke to Renee, and it made me feel less guilty. As I moved toward the seat behind her, the president stopped me, saying, "No, Liz you sit down there in front with Regan."

As I took my seat next to Regan Salina, I tried not to look at the full house of people below, knowing full well they were looking at us. But I couldn't help it. One elderly woman caught my eye and smiled. I smiled back, which seemed to please her. She tapped the man beside her on the shoulder and pointed in my direction. He gazed up with a disgruntled expression as if wondering what I had done to deserve to look down on them as they stared up at me. It was jarring, so I turned my head to Joe, who was sitting behind me beside the president.

They were talking in low voices, and as the lights dimmed, I heard the president say, "Joe, Morrison is getting antsy. I need to make the announcement sooner rather than later."

There was loud applause as the symphony's music director Christoph Eschenbach made his entrance, which prevented me from hearing Joe's response. Then there was the boom of timpani followed by a blast of trumpets—not Rachmaninoff. It was Aaron Copland's *Fanfare for the Common Man*. The kind of boisterous piece which would keep almost anyone awake and entertained.

Joking aside, I was relieved I didn't feel my eyelids getting heavy during the concert. Pretty much anything except for rock and country could put me to sleep, especially in a dark auditorium.

At the conclusion of the program, an announcer asked the audience to remain in their seats while the president and First Lady made their way to the south plaza, where dinner and dancing would take place.

Two secret service agents appeared at the door to whisk us to a tent set up on the south side of the Kennedy Center. There were Chinese lanterns hanging from the tent's ceiling and tea lights floated like lily pads in glass centerpieces on each table. We were the first guests to arrive, and a waiter offered us flutes of golden champagne. The First Lady and I each took one, but the president waved the waiter off as he engaged Joe in a private conversation while a jazz trio played at the far end of the room.

The First Lady asked me where I had my hair done, and when I told her George's, she launched into a story about Rick moving her appointment when she was a senator's wife to accommodate the queen of a Middle Eastern country. Rick told her monarchs beat senator's wives; it sounded like classic Rick. While I knew it was rude not to make eye contact, I couldn't take my eyes off of Joe.

"Joe's one of my favorite people in this city," Regan said, noting my concerned look, "but you should know he's already married."

I almost choked on champagne when she continued, touching my arm gently. "He's married to his job, just like my husband. They're not content making one person happy. They only feel satisfied when they're making hundreds of thousands of people happy."

She cut herself off as we were engulfed by the crowd. I didn't know what to make of what she had said. Of course Joe wanted to make people happy, but I had not gotten the sense he put his job before everything. In fact, I thought just the opposite.

The First Lady donned her public face, introducing me to a Supreme Court Justice and the Secretary of Veteran Affairs before drifting away. One woman even said how impressed she was with my mother's social skills, gathering political figures and journalists for an Off The Record dinner. I kept myself from crying; if only Mom was here to see me. *No matter how much time passes,* I thought, *I will never not miss her.*

Just as I realized I had been left to stand awkwardly amongst an array of powerful people, I felt arms encircling my waist.

"There you are!" Joe said, with a hint of champagne on his breathe. "How did I get so lucky? You're the most beautiful woman here." I turned to playfully scoff at him, but when I saw the smile on his face and the sincerity in his eyes, I felt the words coming out like water spilling from a glass.

"I think I might love you, Mr. Reilly."

Joe took my hand and we glided to the dance floor as the band played Jackson Browne's "Somebody's Baby." "I think I love you too, Miss Mason."

There was no question Regan Salina knew her husband well, but she didn't know a thing about Joe Reilly.

CHAPTER

FIFTEEN

"For most folks, no news is good news; for the press, good news is not news."

—GLORIA BERGER

Joe and I were enjoying the luxury of sleeping in on Sunday until my phone rang at exactly one minute past nine—Granny knew it was impolite to call before nine.

"Hello…," I answered, still half-asleep.

"Oh, dear, did I wake you?" she said, fully cognizant she had woken me up and not caring in the slightest.

"Yes," I said.

"I'm all out of moisturizer and a few other things. Do you think you could go to Saks for me today? You can get yourself a little something."

"Sure I can, Granny."

"That's so sweet of you, dear. I also have a new grocery list for you." I never doubted it for a moment.

"I'll get the list a little later, Granny. When I wake up."

"Oh, I didn't mean to wake you," she said, as if this wasn't a weekly occurrence.

"It's okay, Granny. I'll call you back in a bit...," I yawned as I hung up the phone.

Joe rolled over and put his arm around me.

"So, do I get to meet Granny today?" he mumbled.

"Hmm...," I said, not at all convinced it was a good idea.

"Are you embarrassed by me?" Joe asked. I couldn't think of anything less true. "Do you think she's not going to approve?"

"God, no!" I said. "It's the opposite. I'm completely embarrassed by my grandmother. I love her, but she's crazy."

"She can't be crazier than *my* grandmother. If someone in the neighborhood made her angry, she would call the funeral home and have a hearse sent to their house."

"No, she didn't!" I laughed.

"Oh, yes, she did." Joe lifted his head from the pillow just enough to look me in the eye, "So, are you going to introduce me to Granny, or am I going to have to track her down through the NSA?"

"Fine," I said. "You can meet her. But let's try and get another hour or so of sleep first."

"I'm not interested in sleep," he whispered against my lips, pulling me closer.

* * *

When I woke up a few hours later, Joe was already up and seated at the kitchen island with a coffee and a scowl. That morning's *The Washington Post* was laid out in front of him as he read the sports section with a furrowed brow. He would look frighteningly mad if his glasses weren't perched at the tip of his nose.

"Good morning, Mr. Reilly," I smiled, making my way to the coffee pot. "Any left for me?"

Without even looking at the paper, he recited a headline aloud. "Love crosses West Wing lines. White House chief of staff Joe Reilly has found himself some fresh press arm candy who's somehow even younger than him. The—"

"Wait, wait, wait," I said walking over to him, still in a robe and slippers. "This is in *The Post*?" I knew the answer, but it was almost too hard to believe.

"It sure as hell is. They make me look like I'm forty-five, and you're...twelve."

I walked over and read the article over his shoulders, and he was right. They had taken a photo of me which looked like my high school yearbook photo, and one which displayed Joe's few wrinkles in quite an unflattering light. After a closer look I realized it actually was my high school yearbook photo, making me seventeen. It wasn't a terrible picture. I just didn't look old enough to drink, much less date a man who had security clearance. The article read:

The former New York lawyer, 36, was seen hand-in-hand with DC legend Bennett Mason's granddaughter, Elizabeth Mason, 26, at Saturday night's Kennedy Center Honors. Mason was recently hired as a junior investigative journalist at The District, *while Reilly has just barely got his foot inside the White House doors. Looks like Washington has its very own Romeo and Juliet—but will the political power couple survive in this trustless town?*

Hearing my job title reminded me I still didn't have a storyline for O'Donnell on the bill, or Alicia for that matter. I decided to see if she could be of any more help.

"Does the name Tommy Hall mean anything to you? Might have something."

I messaged her, careful to conceal my phone screen from Joe's eyes. But he was still staring at his own unflattering photo.

"Who died?" asked Casey, stumbling into the kitchen wearing one of my high school t-shirts.

"There's an article about us in *The Post* this morning," I said confidently. I could tell Joe was not entirely psyched about it, but apparently I was one half of a political power couple. Mom would love it.

"Duh," Casey said, pouring herself coffee. "Are you surprised?"

"No, they just make me seem much older," Joe stated, still not looking up from the paper.

"I mean...," Casey droned, and I worried what was coming next. "It's pretty hard to look good standing next to that," she finished, gesturing in my direction. I wasn't one of those rise-and-shine-with-glowing-face girls. We're not talking unsightly. We're talking gruesome: eyes swollen, face blotchy, and my hair had transformed from last night's blow out into something a creature could nest in.

"I think she looks beautiful," Joe teased, after taking a thorough look at my tired features, "even more so than last night."

"Alright, neither of you are getting breakfast," I stammered, as though I was going to cook anything anyways, "and Casey, you have work in an hour. Go get ready!"

"Yes, Mom," Casey whined as she sulked out of the kitchen.

"I sent a driver to get a sweater and khakis for me to wear to Granny's," Joe smiled.

"Ugh. I hoped you'd forgotten about that."

"Nope," he said. "I'm going to change." I looked down at my robe and slippers and decided to follow him. He was acting like we were going on a field trip. I thought about calling Granny and telling her I broke a limb to escape his inevitable disappointment.

She hadn't always been demanding, but after Granny's second husband died she morphed into the role of doting grandmother, which made her feel entitled to demand I dote in return. She spoiled me ridiculously. I got everything from a bedroom in her home with a canopy bed and a doll house when I was young, to a late bedtime so I could stay up and watch "adult" TV shows like *Sex and the City*.

When I was a little older, she let me have boys over to swim in her pool, and turned her head when they brought beer and we played loud music. She was always on my side. Anyone who upset me was a "damn fool," including my mother. But she certainly wasn't the first person in my family I wanted to introduce to Joe. Luckily, Joe had such a great sense of humor about things. At least, I hoped he would find her amusing as opposed to horrifying.

"Ready?" I asked, landing at the bottom of the stairs in a plain white t-shirt and leggings.

"Yup," he said, putting down *The New York Times* crossword puzzle. Finished. In ink.

We headed toward my Jeep in the back driveway. "We have to stop at Saks on the way," I mentioned as we climbed into the car.

"Yay!" Joe teased, "I could use a new Chanel bag."

* * *

No matter how many times I visited Granny's, I was always caught a little off-guard by how suburban looking it was—it's not at all what one would expect in the middle of a "big city" like Washington.

I brought Joe in through the garage and entered the main foyer.

"Granny?" I yelled. "It's Liz!"

"I'll be down in a second dear!" she bellowed from upstairs.

When I turned around, Joe was examining bookshelves in the living room. Some of the items belonged to Bennett Mason, some were my mother's, and then there was Granny's "Green Book" collection.

The so-called "Green Book" is actually *The Social List of Washington, DC.* The book is covered in a distinctive Kelly green felt, hence the nickname. Like every city's social registry, it lists the most prominent old families with their summer home and winter home contact details. But, this being DC, it also lists all the members of Congress, the diplomatic corps, top White House officials, and the Cabinet. Granny had every "Green Book" since 1942 lined up neatly on the back bookshelf behind GP's old office desk. Even though they divorced, she claimed a lot of his items when he died because Mom didn't have any room.

I heard a clicking of heels coming down the stairway and felt my shoulders rise. Granny was taking each step as gracefully as she could, clutching her rat-like dog in one arm and a piece of paper in the other.

"Granny! This is Joe," I said, "Joe Reilly. Joe, this is Granny. I mean, Martha Mason."

Granny looked at him like a starving dog eyeing a filet mignon. "Well, aren't you a handsome thing," she said with a long drawl. It wasn't so long ago I was young, and I would have chased you all over this room."

"Well, if I hadn't fallen for your wonderful granddaughter, I wouldn't have run," he said without missing a beat.

They were flirting. *Unbelievable.* Granny was being totally—and ridiculously—serious, and Joe was happily playing along.

"Granny, the grocery list?" I asked, searching for a chance to get out of there.

"Oh, yes," she said indifferently, hesitating to take her eyes off Joe.

"My list is right here, but I need to explain some things."

"Well, while you ladies go over the list, why don't I take that fine-looking pup out for a breath of fresh air?" Joe offered.

The poor animal probably hadn't seen the light of day in years. Granny's fear of abandonment extended to pets, so she kept them locked inside and wouldn't let anyone else near them. Occasionally, they might get a quick trip out in the evening to the small bricked-in courtyard off the kitchen.

"I don't know...," Granny said, clutching her prisoner.

"I saw a leash in the front hall. Don't worry. I'll just let him wander around the front yard."

Leash? I hadn't seen a leash. The only leash she ever had was the one she kept her late husband on.

"Aren't you sweet," she purred, looking up at him with an expression that was probably alluring about a half a century ago.

"My pleasure," he said as he picked up the animal and headed for the front door. Joe looked pleased with himself. The dog, clearly aware he was being liberated, jumped in Joe's arms, wagging his tail and yelping.

Granny waited until she heard the door shut and got right down to business. Gone was the seductive smile and throaty voice—she was all about strategy.

She began, "Elizabeth, he is divine. Just divine. Now, let's talk about how you keep him. Of course you're gorgeous, brilliant, and he couldn't find a young woman with better genes."

"Thank you, Granny, he is special." We headed toward the kitchen and her tone became even more serious,

"He would be a damn fool to let you go. But if I've learned one thing in my life, it's that men are damn fools. They don't want anything that comes easily. So, let's see. Why don't we start by sending you a dozen roses? No, two dozen. Do it right now while he is outside. You can use my credit card. Don't tell him who they're from. Make him wonder. You have to keep men on their toes."

"Granny, thanks for the idea," I said as graciously as possible. "Normally, it would be very clever. But Joe is the White House chief of staff and I don't really think he wants to deal with fictitious suitors. It's a good idea, really, but not this time."

"White House? He works at the White House?"

Oh no. Why did I tell her that? Of course, it was the only part of what I said that she glommed onto. She would be calling Joe's office with grocery lists now. But then I remembered I couldn't even get through to Joe at work. She wouldn't be able to either. Except she would probably be so insistent, she'd end up on some secret service stalker watch list.

"Yes, but he is never there—always out of the office. Virtually unreachable. You can't even leave him messages," I spoke as firmly as possible.

"I wouldn't dream of calling him," she insisted. *Yeah, right.*

After she explained three times the importance of selecting a carton of milk from the back of the shelf, she relinquished her grocery list, and I checked Wire for any messages from Alicia.

A.M. (1)
"The President's nephew. There's more of a story than you'll find in the tabloids. Meet me for lunch tomorrow, same spot as before."

I typed quickly and headed back into the foyer.

"See you at noon."

Joe appeared through the front door trying to contain Granny's agitated dog. Clearly it didn't want to come back inside. *Shocker.*

"Well, darling, you have my list. I wouldn't mind visiting longer with Mr. Reilly if you would like to head to the grocery store." *I'm sure you wouldn't.*

"That's very sweet of you, Mrs. Mason. I would much rather stay here than go into the office so early on a Sunday, but duty calls."

I knew Joe had a few hours before he was needed at the White House, but of course he managed to both lie and charm my grandmother. I kissed Granny goodbye and she wrestled the emotional dog upstairs. Joe and I headed out to Whole Foods.

"She loved you," I said as we drove away.

"I loved her," Joe said, "and if anything happens between us, it's good to know I have options."

CHAPTER

SIXTEEN

"If you can't get rid of the skeleton in your closet, you'd best teach it to dance."

—GEORGE BERNARD SHAW

I don't remember when it was I became comfortable being alone.

There were a few times in high school and college when my anxiety would get so bad I couldn't bear to be alone. I needed to be in the presence of someone, and I didn't always choose the best company. Eventually I learned how to enjoy being by myself. Sometimes I enjoyed it too much.

It wasn't like I hid from people, or I'd never thought about meeting someone—relationships just started to matter less to me when they started mattering more to everyone else. In college it became exhausting to try and exist happily with people when all I could think about was Mom surviving. It was like holding my breath waiting to be pulled underwater at any minute. But no one else was panicking.

So sometimes I got mad. I got pissed off no one else had to panic. I wanted to wave my arms and scream to get their attention. I wanted to be like them, ignorant and blissful. But by the time graduation came and I was back living with Mom, I found it easier to just disconnect. And I stayed disconnected for a while. If I wasn't at home, I was at Millies. If I wasn't with Mom, I was working. Before I knew it, three years had gone by and I was still holding my breath.

"Knock, knock!" Casey said, tapping on the door frame and lunging herself onto the bed. "You okay?" she squeezed my knee and I snapped out of it.

"Yeah. Just thinking." Casey let out a chuckle and walked over to pick up my hair dryer.

"What?" I inquired.

"Remember the first week you left for school?"

"Vaguely."

"Your mom made me stay here—well, I didn't want to go home. But she wouldn't let me."

I laughed. Casey pretty much moved in after that. "Yes."

"Well, a few nights after we got back from dropping you off, your mom starts running around the house looking for a hairdryer. But then she remembered how you always kept one by your dresser mirror."

"Oh god," I groaned. I knew this story, but I let Casey go on.

"So she waltzes into your room to get it, and when she sees the empty dresser, she just loses it. She's wailing 'Oh my god, she's really gone,' and 'look at how empty her room is.'" Casey impersonated my mother even better than I could, imitating her soft and elegant debutante voice and fascinating facial expressions.

"That's so sad," I said, amused by Casey's performance.

"She wouldn't get off the floor until I mentioned going to Thomas' Sweets. So we drove there and ate peanut butter sundaes in the car on P Street."

"She loved those." I shook my head. "She loved peanut butter on anything."

"And ketchup!" Casey laughed. "I miss El, too. The way she laughed at us. When she would always come downstairs to you and me in our Millies polos, drunk, making frozen pizzas."

"Girls!" I mimicked Mom's voice and the way she shook her ponytail, "could you be any louder?"

"No! And when she'd make us sit at the island and would end up baking the pizzas for us." Casey chuckled, "and I always woke up with a trash can next to the bed."

No matter how many times I brought Casey home and she made too much noise or threw up in the bathroom, Mom loved her because I loved her.

"There will never be another Eleanor Mason," I declared.

Casey nodded. "The world couldn't handle it."

* * *

Casey and I had fallen asleep telling old Millies stories, and when my alarm went off at 7:30 a.m., she groaned and rolled over. *Must be nice*, I thought. I wasn't much looking forward to plopping down into my desk chair next to Derek, but then I remembered Alicia and I had plans at noon. Luckily, I didn't have to ask O'Donnell for a lunch break.

I arrived back at the Hay Adams to find Alicia sitting in the same booth as she did before.

"If you order whiskey again I am not paying," she laughed. "I can tell you about Tommy Hall, but I'm not sure it will get you anywhere. Unless you want to write sleaze pieces at the *Enquirer.*"

"God, no," I groaned.

"Tommy is Emmett's son from his first marriage. I'm sure you read that."

"That, and how he's in the Peace Corps working in Belize."

"Not exactly," Alicia confessed as a server approached us.

"May I have a chamomile tea...and a piece of toast with peanut butter? If you can," she delicately asked. Being stop-and-stare gorgeous *and* pregnant had its benefits.

"Yes ma'am," the server nodded, then turned to me.

"May I please have..." I looked at Alicia for a sign of permission, but her face bore no such thing. "Just a ginger ale? Thank you."

The server nodded and scurried off. "Tommy's not in Belize. He's in Utah." Alicia explained, "When Stephanie and I joined the president's campaign, we asked the Salinas if there were any skeletons in the closet the media hadn't already dug up. They told us about Tommy. He was never in the Peace Corps, but they put that article out in case anyone came looking."

"Emmett and Renee usually don't come to DC. I mean, rarely." I remembered Rhonda said it was because Emmett was jealous. I wondered if Rhonda knew about Tommy.

"Yes, because of Tommy. The less Emmett is seen with the president, the less people care about him. The less people care about him, the less they dig for skeletons." I nodded, and I was still confident in my observation Alicia seemed more like an actress who plays a senior counselor on television than an actual senior counselor.

"Tommy had a drug problem," she continued. "Started as a young teen. First it was coke, and then it was heroin. Eventually, he spiraled out of control."

I could already see the terrible look on Joe's face if I wrote a story about a kid with a drug problem, especially knowing what I did about his mother.

"Anyway, Tommy came home one night about five years ago, long before Mark Salina had his eye on the presidency, and he was completely freaked out—crying, apologizing."

Our server returned with both of our beverages and a beautifully arranged plate of toast with several small jars of peanut butter and assorted jams. I had almost forgotten we were in a restaurant in Washington and not in a political drama series.

"Oh, this is lovely. Thank you so much," Alicia purred. The server blushed.

After spreading a generous amount of creamy peanut butter on one of the toast triangles, she continued in between chewing. "Tommy was still in high school, had been working as a drug mule to pay for his own."

"Jesus Christ," I whispered.

"So he comes home that night bawling and scared half to death. Said the gang found out he'd been stealing. I think he lost a pretty large shipment on a bender, or something like that. Anyway, when Emmett called the president—he was a Texas senator at the time—he told them to stay away. Emmett and Renee picked up and moved to Utah, where they changed Tommy's last name to Renee's maiden name and enrolled him in a rehab program. He's still there."

"Why are Emmett and Renee here now if the president told them to stay away? I just saw them at the Kennedy Center. Can't the president do something?"

"Trust me, we thought of everything. If it came out now the president knew about his nephew's involvement with a drug cartel while he was in the Senate? No. They just have to wait and be careful."

"Poor kid," I sighed.

"We advised the president, when he told us, to rekindle his relationship with his brother to avoid any suspicion. If they didn't have any dialogue, who knows what Emmett would do. So he makes an appearance once a year, and that's that."

"Why hasn't Emmett exposed him? Isn't he pissed he never helped Tommy?"

"That I don't know," Alicia admitted. "Maybe he doesn't want to be the disgruntled family member who insults the president of the United States, or maybe he's protecting Tommy. If they tried to make a deal with the cops, the system would eat him up. Any intel Tommy has is outdated, and the gang has moles."

"So you don't think Tommy is relevant," I confirmed.

"Emmett has no room to blackmail the president. I've thought about it every which way. As far as I'm concerned, he's a screwed-up kid with a bad past. Aren't we all?"

Alicia was fascinating. I nodded and sipped my ginger ale. Part of me never wanted to find anything, so we could meet in this booth and gossip forever.

"Alright, well. Now you have all the skeletons I do. Gotta go." She finished the last of her tea and left the bar holding a piece of toast in one hand and a peanut butter jar in the other. She didn't look like a pregnant lady, but she definitely had the disposition of one.

CHAPTER

SEVENTEEN

"Well-behaved women rarely make history."

—*ELEANOR ROOSEVELT*

If I don't get a latte, someone is getting hit.

I had stayed up until three in the morning trying to find any connection between the president's family and the bill, making me close to fifteen minutes late for work and sweatier than usual. So far, the only storyline I had involved the president's secret nephew with a drug problem

As I approached my still unfamiliar cubicle and squeaky desk chair, Derek was already working. To my surprise, he had brushed his hair.

"Did you see the list of wartime suppliers is out? Well, only the companies they've picked so far." I chugged the remainder of my coffee in an effort to prevent screaming at him.

"Looks like I'm about to," I huffed, slinking into my desk chair and pulling my two-day-old curls into a low ponytail.

"*New York Times*," he offered, and I tried to keep my eyelids from closing as the ancient computer started up. After several painful minutes of waiting, I was finally able to navigate to the most recent *New York Times* article. Sixteen US-based companies were identified as highly plausible candidates for wartime supply production. I only recognized a few, either from watching *Bloomberg* or from a football stadium bearing the name. But one name caught my eye.

Holy shit. I felt my stomach drop when suddenly my feet began to move faster than my brain.

"Liz?" Derek yelled after me, but I was already in the lobby.

My hands were shaking, making it seemingly impossible to dial her cell, but eventually I heard it ring.

"Rhonda. Can you talk?" *Wait. She can't know why you're asking. Calm down.*

"Well hello, little miss *Washington Post*! Are all of your famous friends busy?" she purred through the speaker. *Thanks. I had forgotten I'm dating the chief of staff.*

"Oh please, it was one article," I mustered enough confidence to not sound like the floor was being torn up from under me. "I met the president's brother last night, and he's handsome," *There you go. Keep going.* "He and his soon-to-be-ex certainly fooled me!" I waited for her response and prayed to god my voice hadn't shook.

"Oh, I know! Maybe I have a chance!" Rhonda teased, and I regained control of my extremities.

"Anyway, you're not going to believe this, but I got a letter addressed to Mom from the company you mentioned the other day, the one they're fighting about. I'm pretty sure it was them—what was the name again?" I tried to ignore the fact I'd gotten immensely better at lying since taking up this job.

"Oh gosh, honey…I think it started with an M…Menda something? Menda Corp!"

I slid my thumb to the end call button and let my phone fall onto the bathroom counter. I had figured out why the president was so desperate for the bill to pass, and why equity caused such a big fight in his brother's divorce. With the money MNDA Corp would make through its defense contracts, they could pay off Tommy's debt without anyone batting an eye.

I didn't want to expose Tommy. The kid deserved people to help him. But I hated the president for letting his nephew stay terrified in some Utah rehab center. He had already gotten away with ignoring Tommy's cry for help, but he wasn't going to get away with corruption. If I could find proof of Salina's MNDA Corp equity, it would be enough to at least expose conflict of interest.

But I needed more than Rhonda's shitty memory to corroborate the equity claim.

"Derek!" I shouted. It was a long shot, but I didn't have any better ideas.

"Woah. What?" Derek griped.

"If I wanted to figure out who had equity in a company, where would I start?" Derek turned to look at me like I was speaking another language, before his grimace turned into a grin.

"Oh, you're *not* working on a story about the bill. What'd you find out?"

"Nothing." I shook my head in hopes of being believable. "I'm not asking for a story. I think my mom had shares in MNDA Corp, but I can't find a certificate or anything at home. I just thought you might know stuff about stocks."

"Do you know what brokerage firm she used?" Derek asked with a concerned look. I felt bad for using the sympathy card, but I also knew no one ever assumed Derek was helpful.

He seemed excited. Having no response to his question, I smiled naively and shook my head.

"Well you're gonna have to contact MNDA directly." Derek rolled over to my desk and began typing into the search bar.

"Investor Relations will have a record if she did buy anything. Here," he pointed to a section of the company's annual report. "Call that number."

"Wow. Thank you." I felt my cheeks get hot as Derek rolled back to his desk and resumed whatever it is Derek does. Before I had time to question my plan, I was already on my feet headed for the lobby.

"Wendy, I have to make a phone call, be right back!" I hollered. Wendy smiled and I rounded the corner too quickly to hear exactly what she said. When the elevator doors opened and I exited to the street, I pressed the call button.

"Investor Relations. This is Scott."

"Hi, Scott. This is...Samantha." *Lie.*

"How can I help you?" I did not quite know how to articulate the answer.

"My mother recently passed away, and I remember she bought stock in MNDA Corp. I have searched her files through and through and I can't seem to find any certificate...I just want to account for all of her assets. You understand?"

"Of course, ma'am," Scott replied. "I'm so sorry for your loss."

"Thank you." The guilt was sucking me in like quicksand.

"What was your mother's last name?" I remembered Rhonda said the equity was in Renee's name, but they could not have been dumb enough to keep it under Salina. Then I remembered Tommy.

"Hall. Her last name was Hall."

"Okay, give me one moment." I waited for Scott's voice for what seemed like an eternity, and all I could think about was five black Suburbans pulling up and FBI agents circling me.

"Ma'am?"

"Yes, I'm here," I sighed.

"Alright, I did find two securities in the last name of Hall. If you could give me the first initial we can go ahead with getting you proof of ownership."

"Wow! Thank you so much, Scott. The first initial would be 'R.'"

I heard a few clicks and then he said, "Alright I do have a Renee Hall. Now, if you could just provide me with the last four digits of her social security number, I'd be happy to get you with the information you need."

"Oh shoot, Scott! I'm so sorry, I'm getting a phone call I can't miss. Can I have my accountant call you back another time? Thank you so much for your help. My apologies."

"Oh, sure, okay, not a problem." I clicked off and bit my lip. Scott sounded nice, and I was definitely going to hell.

* * *

I knocked on the door of O'Donnell's office, feeling like a CIA agent had taken over my body. I could no longer keep track of how many times I had lied in one day. But I wasn't finished.

"Hi sir, I have a meeting with a source at 3:00 p.m., and I was wondering if I could work from home afterward? I completely understand if not, I just—"

"This must be quite a story, Liz! How is your piece going?" he practically yelled.

"It's getting somewhere. I should have it to you in the next day or two."

"Alright then," O'Donnell smiled, but his eyebrows were raised with interest, "see you tomorrow." He practically posed it as a question.

I raced downstairs to my car and dialed Alicia's contact on Wire with no response. When I was finally seated in the car and breathing at a normal rate, I texted Rhonda.

"Phone died! Sorry. Call you later."

That's when Alicia messaged me.

A.M. (1)
"In the middle of sonogram. I'm downtown. Want to meet?"

I wondered if I should get out and take a cab or just deal with city parking in rush hour, but then the idea of being in a restaurant—or any public place where people would hear me—made my spine shiver.

"My mother's house is 3 miles from Georgetown. Would you be able to meet me at home?"

I requested, knowing she would understand my desire to avoid public soon enough. In the minute or so it took for my car's air conditioning to cool down, Alicia replied.

A.M. (1)
"Send me the address."

Thank god. I feverishly typed Mom's street address out and then made my way up and out of the garage. It was already hard enough to drive through downtown DC, and my rollercoaster of emotions was certainly not helping.

When I got home, I jumped into the shower and paced the kitchen floor until Alicia arrived. It was nearing 3:00 pm, which meant Casey would be coming home from her afternoon shift in the next hour. Alicia felt somewhat like an imaginary friend, and if Casey met her everything would become all too real. I knew I had to make our meeting quick, so when Alicia approached the front door, all of my intel spilled out before I could think.

"I heard from a friend Emmett and Renee have equity in MNDA Corp. I called the company to confirm it and the stock is under her maiden name. That's why the president was so desperate to get the bill through. With the money Menda would make in defense contracts, his brother could pay off Tommy's debt without raising any red flags."

Alicia paused in the doorway, nodding and looking at me like I was crazy. "May I come in?" she asked.

"Sorry. Of course." She set her purse down on the living room couch and we walked over to the kitchen island.

"Beautiful house," she smiled, admiring the dark, wooden dining room floors and plates of china on the bookshelves.

"Thank you. It's messy, and I have to figure out where everything goes." Alicia gave a look of sympathy, before sitting down at one of the kitchen bar stools.

"So, who's your friend? That told you about Emmett and Renee? I mean—are you sure she's trustworthy?"

"I'm positive. She and Renee go way back. It's likely Renee doesn't even know what's going on. I mean, Tommy's not her son."

"So, you don't even need the conversation I gave you; there's enough evidence now."

"With the proof of Renee's stock in MNDA, there's no need to even mention Tommy." Alicia cupped her forehead in her hands before rubbing her eyes and yawning. She seemed much more tired than the first time we met.

"Alright, Liz. You did it. Now the next few weeks, maybe months for you, are probably going to suck. The good thing is, you have the first amendment in your favor. You're going to be pressed to be a part of investigations, to give up your sources, but you are not obligated to do any of it. My advice is you bring it to O'Donnell and go MIA for a bit. He'll probably hire personal security to protect you. Who knows."

I could feel my hands shaking in my lap. I was scared, and it was no longer the fun, secretive kind of scared. I was truly terrified. I let the wave of fear make its way through me as I contemplated my options.

"Okay. I'm going to bring everything I have to O'Donnell, but I have to tell Joe before it comes out. I owe him at least that, don't I?"

"You owe him whatever you want, Liz. It's your story and it's your career."

"I feel terrible. I have to tell him, Alicia. I love him."

"Okay, but what makes you think he could be involved?"

"I don't know. I can't. But the First Lady said he's married to his job and something changes about him when he talks about the president. I think he sees him as a father figure. Also, woman at the hair salon said her husband thinks Joe's the only one the president trusts and how can he be so close to the president without knowing?"

"Liz. You're rambling," Alicia said calmly. *How could she be calm right now?* "As for Joe, I was that close to the president and it was by sheer luck I was in the room with Morrison and Richards. Joe has been a great look for the White House—he's smart, professional, handsome, likable. I doubt the president would jeopardize that, especially if Joe is as honest as you think."

"Okay," I nodded. Alicia gathered her belongings and slid off of the chair, before laying a hand on my shoulder.

"Everything is going to be fine. You did your job." I patted her hand as a way of showing my gratitude and stayed sitting in the kitchen for a while. I couldn't bear to press play on my life just yet. But if I wasn't going to let love keep me from doing my job, I certainly wasn't going to let fear.

CHAPTER

EIGHTEEN

"If you're going to kick authority in the teeth, you might as well use both feet."

—*KEITH RICHARDS*

"Was that...," Casey followed Alicia with her eyes as Alicia headed down the driveway to her car. We had finished our conversation just in time for Casey to round the corner from the street and into the driveway.

"Yes," I declared. "Don't ask."

"Okay. Weird!" Casey smelled like grilled shrimp and sweat, barely masked by her perfume. Although it was disgusting, it made me miss Millies. Bartending never had me secretly communicating with ex-White House staff in a conspiracy against the president.

"Take a shower. Please," I insisted, shooing Casey up the stairs.

"At least I'm not working for the man!" she shouted back at me. I was most definitely not working for the man. In fact, I was deliberately working against him.

"Okay Mr. Shneebly. You still stink."

It was both a blessing and a curse Casey never cared much to talk about things. I knew I would have to explain everything to her eventually, but I also knew she would have questions I didn't yet have the answers to. While she sang Fleetwood Mac at the top of her lungs in the shower, I brought my computer and every blank piece of paper or sticky note I could find into Mom's office. Not only did I have to lay out everything I knew from Senator Richards to MNDA Corp, I still had to combine it all into a news story worth reading.

* * *

By 7 p.m. I officially had my own crazy wall. Post-its with names, sheets of paper with headline drafts, and even newspaper clippings were mounted with thumb tacks. You want to believe everything on TV is exaggerated, but I looked like Claire Danes in *Homeland.* Except I wasn't hunting down an Al Qaeda terrorist. I was exposing the leader of the free world. It would either start or finish my career.

After reading and re-reading the article over and over again, I finally told myself there was nothing left to edit. The headline was the most important part anyway. My working title was "Salina Family Has Stake in Company Connected to DUST Act," but I could hear my inner critic snoring before I even read it aloud. If I wanted to sound any alarms, I would need to get creative.

"SALINA FAMILY HAS MORE TO GAIN FROM DUST ACT THAN LIKABILITY—AND IT'S NOT JUST CHUMP CHANGE"

Feeling satisfied, I lay back on the navy-blue animal print rug Mom and I picked out together so many years ago. If she were here, we'd be sipping microwaved chai lattes and she'd be telling me story after story about her life. My favorite one was when Mom brought her first boyfriend home and Granny started flirting with him. I would laugh so hard the latte would come out of my nose, and Mom would be laughing too hard to care about the rug. I would tell her about Joe, and admit Granny had flirted with him, too. I would ask her opinion about what to do, and she would say something which would probably irritate me, though she'd be right. Everything would be easier if she were here, but she wasn't. Why did it keep taking me by surprise?

Casey knocked at the door and brought my imaginary moment with Mom to a halt. "Liz?" she said softly.

"Yeah."

"Wanna tell me what's going on?" I most certainly didn't. In fact, I needed a break.

"Tomorrow Case, I promise. Pretty busy right now."

"Okay. I'm headed downtown to meet Brandon and the crew for drinks, wanna come?"

"I'm good! Tell them I said hey," and with that, she was gone and I needed fresh air.

I did what I always did: I ran through the pain. I wasn't much of a runner; I never made it past four or five miles. I never had to work out as a kid, and Mom called me "the Waif" because I was so lean. After the first mile, I realized your body just starts to go numb, you don't feel the cramps in your sides or the constriction in your lungs—it's just tingly. It felt like the mental pain stopped when the physical pain did. So in high school, I ran and ran until thinking about Dad didn't hurt anymore. When Mom got sick, I did it again. It was a mental workout; instead of pushing the pain deep down inside, I could sweat it out.

There I was again, forcing myself up Massachusetts Avenue toward Ward Circle. My route was to go from Mom's house to the cathedral, where she was buried next to my grandfather. From the south entrance steps you can see all of the Mall—the Washington Monument, the Capitol, and the Potomac River. I sat on the limestone staircase for God knows how long—until it got dark. The strength of those buildings, having lived through every war this town has gone through, both on and off paper, just reminded me from where and who I came.

Before pulling myself up to journey home, I pulled out my phone. Some things had to be done like ripping off a band aid. Telling Joe was one of those things.

"Need to tell you something important...Can you make it here tonight? And no, I'm not pregnant."

It was too hot to wear anything with pockets, so I was stuck keeping my phone in my waistband. I jogged back onto the sidewalk of Cathedral Avenue and then turned onto Massachusetts Avenue, and reminded myself GP had said to "write the wrong" over and over in my head on the run home.

When I got home, I checked my phone again to no avail. A watched pot takes forever to boil, and I guess the same goes for cell phones. I had no desire to eat anything. The anxiety was already taking up all the room in my entire body, but I had to try. So I threw a frozen pizza in the oven and poured myself a glass of wine. It felt like I knew the world was ending soon, just not exactly how. After a few sips of chardonnay calmed my nerves a bit, Joe responded.

Joe (1)
"I can be there in half an hour, you ok?"

I was most definitely not okay. A wave of guilt flooded my conscience, even more powerful than the one after my conversation with Scott. Then I thought about Derek, and Rhonda, and the look on Joe's face when I told him. I had used each of these people and crumpled them up into a pile of grudges against me. I felt the lump in my throat, and it hurt like hell. But then I realized I hadn't used Joe, and I hadn't used Rhonda. Like Alicia said, it was sheer luck I was in the right place at the right time. I did what I was supposed to do; I wrote the wrong, I listened to Rhonda, and I followed my instincts, knowing full well I would end up right where I was. At the expense of wonderful, smart, and hard-working Joseph Reilly.

"Key under the back doormat, see you soon."

I replied, hoping an asteroid would hit before he got the chance to arrive. I carried my excuse of a dinner upstairs and placed my phone on the bedside table. No amount of wine or deep breaths could make this anxiety go away.

Almost exactly twenty minutes later, I heard the back door open.

"Upstairs!" I shouted, downing the last bit of chardonnay left in my glass.

Each footstep Joe took up the stairs made my pulse throb harder and harder. I knew I had to tell him the most important thing first.

"Well hello," he said, sitting down on the end of the bed next to me, "Alright Ms. Mason, *what* is going on?" he squeezed my knee and lay back on the bed. If his day at work was hard, I could only imagine how much harder it was about to get.

"Joe, you know I am in love with you. I could tell as soon as you sat down at the bar at Millies." Without saying anything, he turned his head to face me. Those green eyes were only making this harder.

"Tomorrow morning, *The District* is releasing my first article."

Sitting up quickly, he exclaimed, "Liz, that's great! Wow."

"No, you don't understand, I—," my eyes began to water, and speaking felt impossible.

"Hey, hey, what's the matter? This is exciting," he said, calmly caressing my shoulders.

"I know about the president," I wailed, the lump in my throat making my voice crack.

He released his hands and stared me straight in the eye. "Wait, what do you mean?"

"Joe please don't make this harder than it is."

"I don't understand, you know about the president's what?"

I began to sob. I knew he couldn't tell me everything, but I never thought he would play stupid. I wiped my tears with my sleeve and blurted out, "Renee's MNDA Corp equity, Joe." I was finding it hard to look at him, so I closed my eyes and continued. "The president made sure Richards and Uncle Mike would get the bill passed by bribing them with cabinet positions."

"Well, offering them," he corrected.

"Because Emmett and Renee have stake in MNDA Corp. He knew he could force any company to produce supplies."

Joe's face turned to a grimace as he stared at the floor.

"How long have you known?" he finally asked in a sullen tone.

"Since this afternoon."

"Did you know—," he paused, cracking his neck and sighing. "Did you know there was something going on this whole time?"

"I knew there might be. A source approached me—"

"A source?" he interrupted, "a source approached you about the president like this and you didn't think to tell me? When?"

"A few weeks ago."

"Weeks ago!" Joe yelled.

"It's my job, Joe. A source approached me with information and I did my job."

I sat in silence for a minute as Joe paced with his fingers interlocked on the top of his head. I knew it was over. *Just rip the band-aid off.*

"You're right," he said, relaxing his arms by his side and walking back over to me.

"My job is to the office of the president. Your job is to be a watchdog. We can't tell each other when it is or isn't okay to do our jobs."

I nodded, and he held me in his arms for a brief moment. "It sounds like my job has an expiration date."

I smiled, and wiped the last bit of tears from my eyes, "So you're not mad?"

"No." Joe looked at the ground and closed his eyes as if something in him was changing right then and there. "I'm sad, Liz. I know it's pathetic, but it felt for a minute there like I had someone to be proud of me again. The president gave me an amazing opportunity. But he also abused the most powerful job in the world."

"Welcome to Washington," I said in between teary sniffles. "I'm so sorry, and I don't think it's pathetic at all. That feeling never goes away. I just hope you don't resent me."

Joe laughed. "I'm really not mad at you, Liz. I'm pretty impressed—and scared of your ability to do recon. I mean, to hold a poker face for this long? Is there anything else I should know?" he teased, poking my ribs.

"Only that I'm married, but I'll let you recover from this before that story." He looked at me with a curious smirk and we both started laughing.

"So, what are you going to do now?" I asked.

"You said the article comes out in the morning?"

I nodded.

"Who else knows?" he inquired, seeming astonishingly not nervous.

"Me, you, O'Donnell, my source, and the wall of color-coded sticky notes in the guest room."

Joe chuckled, and for the first time since this whole thing began, I felt safe.

"Well, I've got less than ten hours of peace left before my life is pure damage control. I think I would like to go to sleep with my girlfriend."

I lifted the covers and lay my head down, realizing I was positively exhausted. I also wasn't used to this. I wasn't used to things working out even better than I expected. I wasn't used to the universe being quite so kind. Joe kicked off his brown leather Oxfords and lay down next to me, and I thought to myself, *this is what it feels like to be happy.*

"I love you, Joe Reilly," I said, holding his left arm in my hands.

"I love you, too," he whispered, kissing my forehead. "We're gonna be okay."

CHAPTER

NINETEEN

"A strong woman looks a challenge dead in the eye and gives it a wink."

—GINA CAREY

No matter how bad things got, or how little I wanted to wake up in the morning, the sun always came up, and I always kept going. I knew I should be proud of the work I'd done. I knew it was important. But when you have someone there for twenty-six years telling you how amazing you are, and reassuring almost every decision you make, it's hard to be confident on your own.

Mom's bedroom window faced the sun in the mornings, and I woke to feel the golden heat on my cheeks. Joe had likely been gone for hours, but he left a note on the bedside table.

Might not hear from me for a bit. Trains and all. I love you.

Even in the face of absolute uncertainty, he found a way to be charming.

I tried a little harder that morning to brush my hair neatly, and I wore my favorite of Mom's suits. I didn't know if I would ever get the chance to again. Wendy smiled at me as I drifted through the lobby holding a freshly printed copy of my article. O'Donnell seemed like the type to want to read things on paper.

"Liz!" he announced as I knocked and poked my head in per usual. "Have you got the story?"

"Yes, sir." I approached his desk and offered the sheets of paper to him. "I know you wanted a story on the bill. This is about the bill, but it's also about the president. There's conflict of interest sir, it's…not good."

He lowered his glasses down to the tip of his nose and read carefully. I was ready to pack my things and shamefully go home. Then he said:

"Liz. This is not what I sent you out to do."

"I know sir, and I understand if you want to fire me—"

"No Liz, you aren't hearing me. This is more than I sent you out to do. I sent you out to write the wrong. How can I scold you for doing exactly that?"

All I could suffice was a nod. After skimming the article a few times more, he looked back up at me. "How does this all fit in to your relationship?" he asked, and I realized I had forgotten he was also a human who read *Daily Mail* and *The Post.* "You're not required to answer, but Joe is not your source, correct?"

"God no," I huffed.

"Have you spoken to Joe?" he asked, rather concerned.

"I have approached this with the utmost professionalism, Mr. O'Donnell. But it felt awfully disloyal to bring this to you without saying anything. I spoke with him last night. He was understanding. Joe is an honest man."

O'Donnell paused to process my remarks. "You're in a very difficult spot, Liz. I admire your professionalism."

"Thank you, sir."

"I'll get this to copy editing, we can have it up in the next hour or two. In the meantime, you should go home and probably find a place to stay for a while. Once this breaks, Connecticut Avenue will be flooded with news vans awaiting your appearance here. You need to be far away from that. I imagine they will find out where you live as well. Can you handle this?"

I could handle it. I always "handled it." Just never so alone. "I can, sir. I wish I had my mother here, she would know what to do, but I will find the support I need. Thank you so much for everything. Thank you for believing in me, and giving me this chance. I hope it works out well for the both of us."

O'Donnell stood and shook my hand with his right and held my shoulder with his left. "You did good. Bennett Mason would be beyond himself."

* * *

I exited *The District* parking lot for the last time until who knows when and made my way home. Casey would be at Millies, but I couldn't tell her anything there without gaining an audience. I dialed the only person who would know what to do.

"Rhonda."

"Hi, baby!"

"I need to come stay with you for a bit."

"Um. Okay. You're freaking me out," she panted.

"Did Renee ever tell you about Tommy?"

"Her son. The Peace Corps kid."

"Yeah. Well, there's more to that—a lot more. Look, I just handed a story in to O'Donnell that's going to put me in a spotlight. A tough one. So I need to get out of DC."

"Alright, honey." She took a deep breath, "Okay. I'm here."

"See you soon." I clicked off with Rhonda and ran inside to fill one of Mom's beach bags with random clothes and toiletries. Rhonda lived about forty minutes outside of DC in the Maryland suburbs, so I wouldn't be too far away if I forgot anything. When the car was loaded, I put my key in the light for Casey and headed toward Massachusetts Avenue. As I passed by Millies, I suddenly had tunnel vision right into the bar. All I could think about were the news headlines plastered on the bar TVs.

The last time I had felt this much uncertainty was when I got home after college graduation. Mom had stopped doing chemo, and there was no way to tell how much time she had.

The first thing I did then was go into work off shift, and Christian put my dinner on the house. He was never much of a talker, but everyone else talked enough for him to know. Chef was there, which always put a big smile on everyone's face. He went to high school with Mom and they had grown close since I started working there years ago. After eating, I noticed a figure resembling him sitting in a lawn chair on the patio. Before I even made it over, he stood up with a huge grin and a, "Ohhh man! Look who it is!"

He gave me a huge hug and smiled ear to ear, joining me at the bar where I was eating my favorite tacos. I told him I hadn't quite secured a real job yet, so of course, I would be returning to Millies that summer. But after the small talk, I couldn't keep it in. He was family. "Holy shit, holy shit," he said with his hands on his head. He started to cry, but the manly kind of crying where their eyes just get wet and it seems like there are no real tears inside. I knew how much he loved seeing my mom. I think she reminded him of high school, the better days, and I think he loves me so much because I look like her.

Making a screeching sound as it squeezed itself back into my brain, I reeled the thought bubble in just as I rounded Westmoreland Circle into Maryland. It was a perfect goodbye. But no matter how many goodbyes I did that day, I didn't feel like I was leaving anything significant or going anywhere significant. Without Mom around, the world just wasn't nostalgic. I'm not sure how else to explain it.

Sure enough, when I pulled down the long dusty driveway and up to Rhonda's house, a Google alert popped up on my phone screen.

"JUNIOR JOURNALIST AT THE DISTRICT AND GRANDDAUGHTER OF BENNETT MASON HAS JUST OUTED PRESIDENT SALINA FOR FINANCIAL GAINS STEMMING FROM THE DUST ACT."

I wasn't sure if it would be good or bad, but my world was absolutely turned upside down and it would take a lot to flip it back over. I picked up my phone to make one last call, which probably should have been to Joe.

"Case?"

"Yo!" she exclaimed. She hadn't heard yet.

"Hey, *The District* is breaking my first story today. I'm not gonna be living at home for a bit. You'll see on the news later."

"What? Where are you going?" she asked, and I heard a load of silverware being poured out for her to polish. It made me miss when the most stressful part of my day was rolling silverware during the dinner rush.

"I'm staying with Rhonda." I heard her sigh, and I knew there wasn't much she could say. "Take care of the house for me and call her if there's an emergency or anything."

"Alright. You know, if I didn't love you, I'd hate you," she teased, and I chuckled.

"Love you, too."

I hung up and took a deep breath, tossing my phone in my purse and gathering my hastily packed suitcase. I was filled with anxiety, but even more than that, I needed someone to tell me everything would be okay. I needed someone to remind me of who I was and to ignore what other people think. I needed Mom.

When I got inside, I handed Rhonda my phone and told her to write down O'Donnell's cell. He should know where I decided to hide.

"Rhonda, I need to just not go back for a while. I don't want to read anything. Honestly, I'm exhausted." I could feel my eyelids getting heavy, and since I hadn't stopped for coffee that morning, I could easily get right back in bed.

"Okay honey…I don't think anyone would blame you. Whatever Joe is thinking right now, well…Like I always say, he is one of millions. You are one of one."

CHAPTER

TWENTY

"Whoever controls the media, controls the mind."

—*JIM MORRISON*

The problem with running away from your life is eventually you have to return to it.

I wouldn't blame Joe if he never wanted to speak to me again. I up and disappeared with no explanation. But even though I couldn't blame him, I knew it would still hurt.

"Liz, I know you told me not to keep you updated. But Joe's on *60 Minutes.*"

I pulled myself out of bed and followed Rhonda into her living room, her one-story ranch-style house had become my safety bubble for the last month. It was far enough away from DC in the Maryland suburbs where I could effectively escape but could still send Rhonda for extra clothes. The few weeks after my piece was released were astonishingly peaceful. O'Donnell sent a private security company to Rhonda's for the week after the piece came out. But soon enough, the focus had been shifted away from me and we no longer needed them. As I settled into the couch like wet soil, I recognized Joe's voice before even looking at the TV screen.

"Thank you for having me," he said.

"It must have been a shock to you when the article came out. You and Miss Mason were in a relationship, correct?"

"We haven't decided to end anything," Joe responded, "but yes, at the time we had started dating."

"Did you have any idea what Liz was working on?"

"I know Liz always tries to do the right thing. I also knew it was her job to report honestly on the White House."

"But did you know about the story?"

"I did not," he stated confidently.

"Did you have any idea it would lead to everything we know about the president now?" the woman asked. The camera switched from her to Joe, who looked at her with the same disappointed stare he gave me when I broke the news.

"Rhonda, what does she mean?" I groaned.

"Honey...It wasn't just the DUST Act where the Salinas slipped up. After they organized an independent counsel to look into the MNDA Corp allegations, well...the floodgates were opened."

"More?" I asked, pulling myself to sit up straight.

"President and Emmett Salina have been pulling stunts like this for decades," Rhonda said, and I pinched the skin on my arm to make sure I wasn't dreaming. *Did she say decades?*

I shot up and headed for the guest room where I'd unpacked the few things I brought with me, with Rhonda scurrying behind. "Do you have my phone?" She halted her scurrying and receded back into the living room. It wasn't hard to throw everything I had brought with me into my suitcase. When I headed to the bathroom to gather my toiletries, Rhonda returned.

"A lot has happened since you left the city. Why don't you let me drive you home and you can see for yourself," she offered, handing me my phone.

"Do you see what I mean?" Rhonda asked, while turning onto River Road.

"MNDA Corp was just the tip of the iceberg," I responded, scrolling through headline after headline which unveiled a plethora of Salina skeletons. One even mentioned me.

"HOW A ROOKIE JOURNALIST'S FIRST EXPOSÉ LED TO THE DISCOVERY OF PRESIDENT SALINA'S CORRUPTED PAST"

I was no longer just Bennett Mason's granddaughter. I was a journalist, and being a rookie made it sound even better. There was one thing I couldn't wait any longer to check, and putting off knowing would only make it worse. So, I typed "Tommy Hall" into the search bar and held my breath as it loaded. I assumed he'd still be in rehab, maybe jail, or even dead. But when I scrolled through the list of results, only one article mentioned Tommy Hall.

"MILLIONS UNCOVERED IN ACCOUNT TIED TO SALINA'S CORRUPT SENATE ACTIONS."

"A bank account in the name of Thomas Hall has been uncovered, where sources say the Salinas have stashed millions of dollars obtained from Mark Salina's various schemes. Thomas "Tommy" Hall is the son of Emmett Salina, and the nephew of President Salina. Tommy's whereabouts are unknown, as well as why the bank account is in his name. It is believed the Salina's profit from MNDA Corp would have been placed in this same account."

"Jesus." I had to call O'Donnell. Wendy would answer if I called *The District*, and I was not about to walk right into her flood of questions. I tried his direct line. After it rang twice, his familiar boastful tone came through the speaker, "Elizabeth! I guess you've come out of hiding."

"I have. I've read the news—well, part of it."

"Every media company in the district—hell, the country—released a piece about you."

"I don't suppose I want to read all of those," I mumbled.

"Well, are you heading back into the city?"

"I am. I'm going back home."

"Your job awaits you. I think it's fair to say you've earned your White House credentials." He let out a big belly laugh and I couldn't hold back a smile.

"I will see you in the morning, then. Thank you, sir."

* * *

I suppose if there was one thing less likely than me feeling excited to see Derek, it was him being excited to see me. I contemplated what sarcastic greeting was awaiting me as I passed Wendy in the lobby. She made a clapping motion with her hands and smiled broadly. Neuroticism and all, her positivity was contagious. I passed O'Donnell's door and rounded my cubicle wall. Oh, how I had missed my squeaky desk chair. To my ultimate surprise, Derek practically leaped out of his chair to hug me.

"Liz! Oh, it's good to see you." He laughed awkwardly, "I mean...You know, someone. It was getting boring around here."

"You too, Derek."

"Have you seen the wall?" he asked, finding his seat again and motioning down the hallway. *O'Donnell's newspaper timeline.* I couldn't believe it. I gave Derek a curious smile and headed toward the hallway of frames. I felt like a kid in an art museum who so desperately wants to touch the sculptures but knows better. Sure enough, when I got down to the far end, the last and most recent headline was from *The Washington Post.* They had written a story on my piece and, thankfully, did not use my high school yearbook photo. It was, for lack of a better word, badass.

"Who ruined my surprise?" announced O'Donnell, parading down the hallway to meet me. I smiled graciously at him and turned my sight back to the article.

"So, what's next?" he teased. "Very good work, Liz. Very good. I can practically see the look on Bennett's face if he were here. Your mother, too."

"It's a good thing my mother never had the Salinas over for dinner," I marveled. O'Donnell laughed.

"What is next?" I asked, realizing it was a question much more for myself than for him.

"I believe there's some catching up you need to do on recent events," he replied, "and then, well, it's up to you. I'm sure there is still unclaimed territory with regard to the Salinas' history." If there's one thing I did not want to do, it was go backwards. Plus, anything and everything Salina had touched was already being torn apart by every other media hound in the city.

"I'll have to get back to you on that."

I spent the remainder of my workday greeting fellow co-workers who I had barely gotten to know earlier and reading every article I had missed over the past few weeks. When I pulled into Mom's driveway, Casey was locking the backdoor in her Millies uniform. I whisked my phone out of my purse, called Christian, and rolled the window down to wave Casey over.

"Christian, it's Liz."

"Dizzy...Miss...Lizzie. Welcome back," he chuckled.

"I was wondering, if you aren't fully staffed tonight, I'd really like to come in."

"Yeah...," he sounded like he was scanning the servers on shift. "Why not? See you in an hour," and clicked off.

"Hey stranger!" Casey yelled from the back porch. I hurried up to meet her and she practically knocked me over with a hug.

"Wait for me," I panted, "gotta go change. We'll walk together."

"You're kidding? Right on!" she hollered, and I was already inside.

The August heat would have been unbearable if I wasn't so ecstatic to be back at Millies. Absolutely everything else may have changed, but not the person I was in my navy polo and khaki shorts. Brandon smiled from the bar as I headed to drop my things off in the back office.

"Christian!" I exclaimed. "How are you?"

Without missing a beat, he replied monotonously, "Best day of my life," and just barely hid a smirk behind his sarcasm as he drifted past me through the kitchen. I may have been in the paper, but I was still that over-excited high schooler he hired because she "liked the music they played."

Soon enough, Brandon and I were back to pouring beers and making small talk with customers. The orange bar lights romanticized my inevitable whiskey buzz, "So Far Away" by the Dire Straits came on in the background, and I swore there was nothing else I would ever need in the whole world. Until

I remembered Joe, who was probably dealing with a lot of trains on his own right about now.

I kneeled down under the cash register to pick up my phone, but when I got back on my feet, a familiar face rounded the corner once again. It was Joe, and he was smiling. He didn't look like the mysterious recovering lawyer I had met months ago or the dashing and impressive White House chief of staff. He looked, for lack of a better word, like home.

He pulled out the same barstool he did those many months ago and chuckled at my surprise.

"Casey told me," he admitted. Sure enough, when I saw her standing over by the host desk, she winked.

"The name's Joe Reilly," he offered, reaching his hand out over the bar. I was visibly at a loss of what to say when he continued, "Can we start over?"

I shook my head with a sigh of relief. Starting over was exactly what we needed: a second chance not narrated by the writers of *The Washington Post*. So, I reached my hand out to meet his. "Yes. But this time, off the record."

ACKNOWLEDGMENTS

My tenth-grade history teacher had the same tradition every year: he made sure each student left his classroom with a unique book recommendation. His name was Mr. Hanson, and my recommendation was *Outliers* by Malcolm Gladwell.

The book explains why the Beatles became the Beatles, why Bill Gates was the one to found Microsoft, and why champions of their field become champions: practice. More specifically, at least ten thousand hours of practice.

What I learned from reading *Outliers* is that while all of these champions were outliers in their field because of thousands of hours of practice, not a single one of them could have made it alone.

Less than a year ago, the idea I would write a book at all did not exist. I suppose I had exhausted my checking of all other social media because I consciously decided to look at my LinkedIn messages. Eric Koester, a Georgetown professor and founder of the Creator Institute, had messaged me about his course for student authors and asked if I would be interested in joining. I responded to Eric, as the most articulate of professional people do, saying, "This sounds totally awesome."

We spoke on the phone later that week as I walked to my Latin class in the freezing cold January morning, and the journey that would become *Off The Record* began.

Throughout my writing process, I constantly had to remind myself if I wrote in a character, they needed to serve a purpose. Just as each and every person in our lives serves a purpose.

I owe mountains of gratitude to the kick-ass women who have been both second moms and incredible role models to me since I can remember. Thank you Jennifer Griffin, Norah O'Donnell, and Nancy Cordes for making me believe in my journalism dreams. Thank you Kate Bennet for helping me figure out how to start this book, Stephanie Cutter for helping me figure out how to end this book, Dana Bash for making sure I followed through with this book, and to all the Wobbles for always being there.

Thank you to Reilly—my best friend, my sister, and the other half of the tornado—and Suz, for putting up with me and always being there.

Great thanks to my editor, Kristin Gustafson, and the entire NDP publishing team for never giving up on me even when I missed literally every deadline. Seriously. I don't think they will laugh at that.

Without the incredible support and inspiration from Dean Susan King, Erskine Bowles, Dr. Charlie Tuggle, Dr. Gerald Boarman, Bret Baier, and Gloria Riviera, I would not be studying at the best school in the country. I feel the most pride and joy being a UNC student.

To the late Christian Broder for giving me a job at Millies. "Best day of my life." It was a blessing to know him when I did and the family he built at Millies forever changed my life. Thank you to Manny for putting up with me even when I stir the pot.

To Dr. Boarman and Wendy Sturges, thank you for giving me the chance to go to Bullis. Thank you to all of my incredible Bullis teachers—Mr. McGowan, Mr. Hanson, Mrs. Lombardo, Mr. Rau, Ms. Vellenga, Ms. Gray, and Ms. Martin—for guiding me to become the nerd I am today. You are superstars. Rock on.

Mr. Green and Mrs. Beckmann, *Multas Gratias.* *Insert sarcastically*

Most of all, I want to thank my parents, Jack and Susanna Quinn. Thank you, Mom, for bringing me into this world and doing your best to destroy anything in my way. You taught me everything I know about life, kicked stage three ovarian cancer in the ass, all while building an incredible network of people I can turn to in any situation. Yes, I mean any situation. I'm talking to you Jamie, Sarah, Kristin, Thorp, Alex, and Kathy.

Jack, no one does being a dad better than you do, and not just because you have a bunch of kids to prove it. Thank you for picking up all of my frantic calls and very calmly, very nicely, answering my stupid, I-haven't-slept-in-days questions (i.e. "Is bribery like...illegal? Or just frowned upon?" and "Wait, Google says senate terms are limited, but they definitely aren't...They totally aren't...Right?") You have done nothing but support me my entire life. Well, except correcting my grammar. But hey, that paid off!

Thank you to Ruth, for keeping me sane. Thank you to Nisa, for keeping me sassy. Thank you Natalie and Eliza, who inspire me with their strength every day. Thank you, also, to my best friends Maddie, Julia, Celeste, and Caitlyn, for showing me what it means to care.

Finally, to Liz: thank you for giving me a sense of purpose. I will miss living through you.

Made in the USA
Middletown, DE
14 February 2021

33743629R00109